FC

DISCARD

PERE GIMFERRER

FORTUNY

Translated by Adrian Nathan West

A Verba Mundi Book

David R. Godine · Publisher · Boston

This is a Verba Mundi Book
Published in 2016 by
DAVID R. GODINE, *Publisher*
Post Office Box 450
Jaffrey, New Hampshire 03452

For information, contact
Permissions, David R. Godine, Publisher,
Fifteen Court Square, Suite 320,
Boston, Massachusetts, 02108.

LIBRARY OF CONGRESS CATALOGING-IN-PUBLICATION DATA
Gimferrer, Pere, 1945–
[Fortuny English]
Fortuny / Pere Gimferrer ;
translated from the Catalan by Adrian West ;
introduction by Octavio Paz.
p. cm.
ISBN 978-1-56792-550-0 (alk. paper)
I. West, Adrian, translator. II. Title.
PC3942.17.I5F6713 2015
849'.9354—dc23

2015024958

LLLL institut
ramon llull

FIRST PRINTING
Printed in the United States of America

To Maria Rosa

En ce temps-là on s'habillait de couleurs

TALLEMENT DE RÉAUX

. . . un or
agonise selon peut-être le décor . . .

MALLARMÉ

It is the art of culture, of reflection, of intellectual luxury,
of aesthetic refinement, of people who look at the world
and at life not directly, as it were, and in all its accidental
reality, but in the reflection and ornamental portrait of it
furnished by art itself in other manifestations; furnished
by literature, by poetry, by history, by erudition.

HENRY JAMES

PROLOGUE

The Fatal Weave

OCTAVIO PAZ

Last week I reread *Fortuny* by Pere Gimferrer. Each of the book's brief chapters is an introduction: a few spare phrases trace out a setting and figures that vanish when the page is turned. The book is a kind of visual album wrought with words; leafing through it – reading it – we hardly take note of the textures: moved by curiosity and the desire to see, we scurry off in pursuit of the images. The quest is in vain: they vanish just as they appeared, without leaving any tracks behind. Landscapes, plazas, bedrooms, salons, alleys, parks, men and women (all of them disguised, even when they are naked): we do not see them, we disentangle them, and as we disentangle them, they disappear.

All these settings possess, at one and the same time, the immobility of fixed perspectives and the instantaneous, fleeting character of cinematic images. Each chapter is a painting and a fragment of a film. A painting, because of the book's artistry – almost always energetic: scant lines, but expressive – and, above all, imbued with colors and tonalities, often vehement, at other times nearly extinguished, though in the midst of their withdrawal, the shadows give off brief and violent glimmers. A fragment of a film because of the speed of the images, the way one transforms into another or dissolves on the page (and in the reader's mind). Painting and cinema: a book to be seen, not thought. But seen through the act of reading. Images composed not of lines, forms, and colors, but of words and phrases.

Gimferrer's prose is the prose of a poet. In his poems, among them some of the finest being written in Spain and America today, whether in Spanish or Catalan, I was astonished from the beginning by the presence of an unmistakable language. And that is what distinguishes the true writer from the rest, like the plumage of a bird or the mane of a lion. A language dense, but not clotted, sumptuous but not excessive. A language rent by sudden bursts of passionate or spiritual clarity, reminding me of the heavens of those Venetian painters, split in two, like a fruit, by the light of a final sun. Gimferrer's prose possesses this same density, which harbors a hidden violence. But beyond that, it is rapid – an extremely modern, if decidedly un-Venetian, trait. The speed of his prose comes from cinema, of which he is a devotee and about which he has written insightfully. To say cinema is to say montage, and montage is the governing principle of *Fortuny*'s appearances and disappearances. The text breaks down and coalesces through a series of introductions; taken together, they make up a performance. About what? About Venice, or about Fortuny? It would be more precise to say that the true protagonist, stepping in and out of the hallucinatory theater, is memory itself.

The velocity of Gimferrer's prose – one of the swiftest I know among writers working today – does not permit one to see, on first reading, the combinations of words and syntax, the weave and the diversity of its linguistic revelations. A second reading reveals another affinity: not with cinema or painting, but with tapestry. Every chapter may be viewed as a vignette in a sumptuous fabric. But this tapestry shows nothing, nor does it tell us a story: it is rather a weave of words. The scenes that pass before the reader's eyes lack the continuity of a linear plot: they are simply diffuse figments of narrative. What links them is not continuity but juxtaposition: there is no unifying action, only coincidence of time and place. They are shards of time, or, more correctly, of times. I use the plural because, in Gimferrer's book, as in so much modern writing, time has ceased to be successive and is dispersed in vivid, finite fragments. Though each of these has its individual life, all are moved by a nameless will that intertwines them with others, which in turn reflect or are reflected in them. The same occurs with space: it is also discontinuous and plural. A diffusion of fantasmal Venices and Viennas on the page. Broken dates and places, reduced to particles, fleeting and incandescent.

Every bit of space-time, every scene and every episode, is discrete and unique, but as they intertwine and evaporate, a new figure arises to mark their re-emergence. An unending metamorphosis, resolved in continuous repetition. The chapters are playing cards Gimferrer throws down upon the table of the page; as they fuse, they constitute a figure. *Figure* is the term I use for the people and characters who file past in *Fortuny*, because they want for substance; their consistency is volatile, or better said, it is reduced to simple appearance: amalgams of reflections, which are verbal compositions, intertwining words. The figures are names. Because they are names, they are talismans: it is enough to utter them to call forth other phantoms, other phantasmagorias. They possess a certain power, but that power is of loss: the images they call forth are chimeras that drift away. What is left? What is left, on the page, is words.

PROLOGUE

The book's unity lies not in the story but in the weave. I mean this literally: the warp and weft of words. Tapestry as dynamism: a litany of countries, places, events, figures emerging from forms and colors that are finally nothing but texture. A fabric of sounds and traces. By weave I also mean intrigue: an artifice or conspiracy that draws us in, traps us, leads us astray. The weave of words announces a setting: an arrangement of lines and colors that becomes, little by little, a stage filled with figures; the drawing comes to life, showing itself to be a configuration of fates: a destiny. The weave of words is a fatal trap in which, attracted by desire and death, every figure that appears in Gimferrer's book falls: painters, writers, courtesans, actresses, politicians, designers, characters from fiction and theater. Names, faces, fates: the verbal tapestry is a moral allegory.

FORTUNY

The Man in the Turban

The long black hair of the odalisque unfurls in the dense, stagnant air. Her nude body reclines across a white sheet that spreads outward, engulfing the fabric beneath it, of a profuse and vivid red. Further up, high above the odalisque's head, there hangs a dark green curtain. The odalisque offers up her body, as she offers up the open palm of her hand. An Arab in a turban sits at her feet. A bangle winds around the odalisque's ankle and she gazes upward, scrutinizing the emptiness of the chamber. The crestfallen Arab strums a stringed instrument in the parsimonious darkness. Despite the shadows cast by the turban, the milky glinting of light, and the general murkiness of the chamber, the viewer seems to see the Arab's face.

As one draws near, the face seen up close gives the effect of a face seen from afar; but seen from afar, we know it to be nothing more than the idea of a face. The oil, a bit darkened over the desiccated cardboard, lacks the brilliant, waxen clarity of fresh varnish.

A painting is an autonomous space; but this autonomous space itself inhabits another visible space, in a concrete location. One with curtains, and brocade tapestries, and dark, heavy velvets thick with the suffocating layers of dust from a luxury now centuries dead, founded on petrified splendors and one day paralyzed. Thus the light of Rome crosses the garden with its classical statuary and settles on the white hat of the young woman – we know she is young, but we do not see her face – reclining on a swing, leafing through an album while speaking courteously to another woman seated before her, both vast and tenuous in her aeriform crinoline. In the half-light of the chamber, as with glimmers of flame at once faint and terrible, burns a jagged assemblage of lances and helmets; the feudal glinting of a suit of armor, a shield, an axe; the blind, immobile garb of a tartar horseman, seasoned in the open air, sun-dark from the torrid or snow-capped dunes, come down from the flickering depths of centuries to rest beneath a shelter of shawls overlaid with Coptic imagery and the carved wood of the paneled wall. There is an iron stove with a periscopic pipe, and a painting in the manner of Goya hidden on the wall, among the suffocating tapestries. The chisel of visible space has also chiseled into time, into the brilliance of this morning in 1870.

We didn't see, or thought we didn't see, or saw and didn't realize it, the face of the Arab seated at the odalisque's feet; nor do we now see particularly well the faces of the other two Arabs. There is a courtyard with one wall of ochre and another of white; or else, a white barrier and the ochre ashlar stonework of a larger building, perhaps the tower of a Moorish castle. An Arab in a bluish hat holds up the hoof of a mule while another Arab, kneeling on the the parched earth, brick-red and fissured, nails a horseshoe into place. The standing Arab is little more than a bronze nude grading into olive green; the face of the Arab blacksmith beneath his red turban is scarcely more than an arid smudge the color of a stump of chestnut. More or less like the Arabs of today; but whereas the sky in the courtyard where they were shoeing the mule was of a milky white like mist, the sky here presents a broad horizon with traces of thin blue clouds that vacillate from white to mauve, half-blended, at times, with the more diffuse clouds of smoke from the confusion of musket-fire and the dust kicked up by the Arabian horses thrown into a gallop on the mountain-ringed flatlands of Tétouan.

The uniform jackets of the Spanish cavalry are blue; the officers wear red pants and golden epaulettes, and brandish the white streaks of their unsheathed sabers, slicing the thin, dry air over an immutable background of imperious blue. Plunging in a single blurred breath down into the desolate and bitter scree, this incongruous multitude arrested in instantaneous movement, this band of Arabs dressed in white or green or red or yellow, or in a color that seems violet under the reddish standard tossed by a flamboyant blast of wind, this mass of riders has also not quite been endowed with faces. Terse in the incandescence of motion, they are all moment, a rapture of fulgid colors.

Their movement demands enormous patience with a minuscule paintbrush. The man who wields it – the man who, when he dies amid the exotic, malarial luminosity of Rome's environs, will not yet have finished this painting – we see in profile, bent over an easel bearing a diminutive canvas; one grander, perhaps, for its minuteness, as though it were the last redoubt of color. The man – Mariano Fortuny y Marsal – is seated in the same rocker where the young woman in the white hat had sat before. In the hovel of the odalisque's bedchamber, in the village where the mule is being shod, amid the anfractuosities of Tétouan, the Arabs are faceless. The *contino*, the count-in-waiting, languid in his riding jacket with his small sword and blue gaiters, may have a face, standing in the park against a stone balustrade carved with grotesques, beneath a whisper of exultant clouds – a harlequin of silk in an Italian garden, rendered in watercolors, and looking as if he himself were entirely made of water. Mariano Fortuny y Marsal may have a face as well: not attired as a Roman, or disguised as a Moor with a musket and leather boots, or dressed in the manner of the eighteenth century, contemplating a vase from Arabia, or in the sepia luminosity of photographs, but rather in a canvas painted by Federico de Madrazo, the father of the young woman in the white hat. Federico de Madrazo is a slender man with a dour moustache and eyes that form precise bull's-eyes under the gelid rondure of his spectacles. In the canvas of Federico de Madrazo, Mariano Fortuny y Marsal has black hair and wears a black jacket; the collar of his shirt is white, and a thin gold watch-chain trails from his vest pocket. Mariano Fortuny y Marsal looks back at his viewer from within the painting, his head askance. His hair is tangled by a powerful unseen wind; beneath his collar, nearly grazing the picture frame, his cravat is a scarlet smudge, a yellow haze, a mingled tempest of indistinct colors set alight.

We are living in the ephemeral glory of light in the Roman November, which from time to time gives promise of the sweetness of May's radiance. In the background, the naked bust of a goddess suffuses the garden with whiteness; under the chaste velvet spears of the cypresses, the young woman with the white hat, sheltered by a parasol, feeds on fluid clarities in transverberation. Only a few years back, amid the satin of the September sky in Paris, with parchment-yellow lighthouses on the bridges waylaid by green or blackish waters, Federico de Madrazo also painted a portrait of his daughter Cecilia, the young lady in the hat so white. From outside, all was compact and golden in a gloom of conic roofs and chimneys of sacred soot and imperial cornices stripped bare by the solemnity of daybreak under a cold white sky, dense and untrembling. Not a quiver in the stifling golden light of the Parisian September, which grazes – indeed, as if we were strumming a smooth string – the bobbin lace that adorns the picture window.

Cecilia de Madrazo in Paris, around September of 1867, has somber, tender eyes and a golden cameo on her breast, and a white blouse with trim, and a red shawl with green markings that covers her shoulder, and a black scarf around her neck. On her lips, on her cheeks, a slight, pure touch of pink. In days to come, this face will become another face. In Granada, with spurs of calcareous light in the coruscated gardens, Mariano Fortuny y Marsal will paint the lady of the castle on her deathbed. Upon the blue cushion is a yellowed face edging toward olivaceous; in the depths, the fabric is red, but the chamber turns dark and purple around the inanimate noblewoman with the black hair. Now – many years later – on her deathbed, Cecilia de Madrazo, wrapped in the suffocating luxury of ornamental tapestries, will be nothing more than whiteness beneath the bright flowers: a lily suffused with flickering ice.

The man who photographed Cecilia de Madrazo takes a few steps back in the desolate chamber, imposing in its silent immensity. The man who has photographed Cecilia de Madrazo so many times may also take a few steps back in time. He has a face, we see his face: he is wearing a turban. The Arab from the odalisque's sordid and suffocating seraglio, the ruddy-skinned Arab shoeing the mule, the Arab with the musket riding horseback through the outskirts of the tumult of Tétouan, are all now one man, with a man's face, painted and unpainted countless times in the radiance of the ancient Roman studio. The man with the turban, in this photograph, is not an Arab: he is a European, with black eyebrows, white

5

beard, a kerchief knotted around his neck, and a black-and-white striped djellaba, very broad and roomy in the shoulders. The man with the turban and the djellaba looks at us: he is Mariano Fortuny y Madrazo, in the Palazzo Orfei, in Venice, around 1935.

The Outsiders

No one looks at the two men speaking English, at the two men falling silent in English. It is rather they who look at the others, who look beyond the others, who gaze on the imagined day within the physical day from the shelter of the undulate loggias on the Piazza San Marco. The two men speaking English – John Singer Sargent and Henry James – are emerging from the mahogany-tinted murk of a sitting room. In the Palazzo Barbaro, the eye of John Singer Sargent has come to rest on a pampered panoply of shimmering specters, the Curtis family: under Murano crystal chandeliers, the son-in-law wears white pants and a dark jacket, and the daughter-in-law, in a long pale dress, holds in her hand a cup of tea. Seated in the foreground, the lord and lady of the house: the lady, quite old, stares back at us, a grimace on her heron-like lips, and the old man, grey-haired and drowsy, leafs through an album. Silken and luxurious in the depths of the canvas, the darkness floods the scene with indistinctness.

In the Piazza San Marco, Henry James observes the faultless splendor, of porphyry and marble, of twilight in summer: quite luminous, warm, and clear. In flight from visibility, there is a stream of greenish waters, now splashing, now silent, and a ramshackle and creaky palace in the corridors of the mind, like a storeroom full of damp wood. A palace on the white page, a palace on the scrawled-upon page. Two women live there, like a pair of gutta-percha birds. The older of them, a sterile priestess, her past worn away, erased, and written out again on the calcified wall of the original memory, like the mossy tidemark on the staircase at the base of the precarious gothic edifice; the younger, a turtledove, or rather goldfinch, under cover of the iconic darkness, totemesque or tomblike, of her superannuated consort. The outsider will be someone like himself, someone like Henry James. He asks, amid the porticoes, against the contre-jour of mauve and the naked, shadow-dotted stones of the pearlescent courtyards, for a notion of a simulacrum of life to distend over the soft white clarity of the written page; the outsider will beg the doyenne's withered sterility and the docile suppleness of the youth for a funerary offering, incubated in darkness, purblind and miry as the canal: the secret papers of a dead man, Jeffrey Aspern. From London, the great vulture of dossiers, collector of dust-laden posthumous rarities, has glimpsed the glow of flesh.

At this hour, on an extraordinarily clear spring evening, you will detect in the silence, coming down a narrow canal, the stifled sonority of the oar blows as the black prow of the gondola cleaves the water's stately shimmer. It does not reach the Piazza San Marco. Seated on the terrace of the Florian, the two men speaking English hear, under the slow, luxuriant twilight, the frayed pomp of the café's summer orchestra. Inwardly, perhaps, Henry James is harboring other images. It is rare, in recent years, that the splendor of the cliffs of old England emerging from the radiant, bustling haze, before the deck of the vessel departed from the continent, has left his thoughts. It is rare that he has opened a closet, a wardrobe, going to retrieve a suit laid away, without a ghastly scene flashing before his eyes: the memory of a man shut up in an asylum. With black hair, and greenish skin, covered only by a sheet of coarse linen, the internee passes his day seated on a bench, facing the inhospitable wall. That man – that form – was he: beyond the horror, it was the I of a person who went by the name of Henry James. To write is to transcend, to overstep the limits, it is to extend the margins of horror. The palace's inhabitants are hinges that give a glimpse, like a shade that filters a light too bright, of the spark of panic, the night of the suffocating, vertiginous closet.

They arrive – the younger woman and the collector – from the far side: from the direction of the Piazzetta, coming up the quayside, on foot, brusque after stepping down from the gondola, soon with their backs to the great sheet of quicksilver, in the direction of San Giorgio, walking parallel to the sawtooth lace of the Palazzo Ducale. The piazza is also, in the soft light of the porticoes, a place of intimate shop-windows that shimmer like the filaments in bulbs. A place of temptations and confusions: in the frames of the display cases, in the flickering of the swordplay of the word, in the calligraphy of space, in the vicinity of the onlookers at the gilded dusk. Something crumbles, something slips away from line to line, from one word to the other; something vanishes amid the indecisions and incisions and the intimations of the summer crepuscule. Something – and one had to confront it with the equanimity of light in autumn and the measured indifference of London's austere darkness – was also disquieting and transitory in the furnished room at 3 Bolton Street, deep in the heart of Piccadilly, when Henry James, out for his afternoon walk, would happen, at times, upon John Singer Sargent, wandering beneath the waning sky. The sound of the orchestra of San Marco is vague and vacant in the calm, erratic air.

The eyes of Henry James do not change with the passing

years: they are always steady and cavernous, vigorous and tender. Beneath his top hat, with great rings under his eyes, etched by time into his face's faultless flesh; clean-shaven, with a touch of weariness, and a defiant, unabated luster; or else redressing his baldness with a black beard, concealing the polished whetstone of his chin, firm and faint as the flourish, when he signs documents in Venice, that prolongs the *S* of his surname into an arabesque at once jab and filigree, pressing upward from the pale bottom of the page. It presses upward thus; implacable, impeccable, and delicate, the wall of this verbal edifice: the history of an outsider who, one summer afternoon, on the terrace of the Florian, asks a young girl for the papers of Jeffrey Aspern. When they return to the canal, the air has grown dense; beneath the window, arrested in the darkness, the gondola glides by, its course immobile and chimerical. The mirrored image of a lighthouse shimmers over the swaying, mirrored surface of the water.

At this moment we may read the story; it has the scent of ink about it, the shrill, abrasive memory of printing presses. Henry James and John Singer Sargent are no longer seated on the terrace of the great café. In Venice, in 1889, in the Palazzo Ca' Rezzonico, shielded from the empyreal gold of the abandoned ballroom like another shadow in the sedan chair, Robert Browning, who dreamt, in a poem never heard, of the clashing of an intangible toccata with masks and sabers in the scintillating night, has died. Mariano Fortuny y Madrazo is living with Cecilia de Madrazo in that scarp of Venetian silver, the Palazzo Martinengo.

A few months back, the world learned the turbid, stifling tale of the Aspern papers. At daybreak, in the piazza, there is no one: a diaphanous goblet of water. The light is clear and naked in the air, shimmering like a sword.

The Flower Maidens

The man has seen the flower maidens. It is a peach-pink winter morning when the wind grows more piercingly cold. Under the clock tower – tolling in the heights, its bronze gone green – shine the damp flagstones of the Piazza San Marco. Liquid sky in aqueous light. Taking a few steps beneath the porticoes, we will see, at the other end of the square, the lamps of the Florian, which at night were a violet luminosity; and our eyes may catch a glimmer of the lambent red upholstery behind the windows of the great café. The flower maidens shield and unshield their bodies, all verdant clarities of flowing sap, of pollen and dew at daybreak. The flower maidens lead astray, in the moral thicket of allegorical disputes, the unblemished swain, the squire with the golden hair. The flower maidens, ivy and lichen, lead Parsifal astray.

It is here that he is accustomed to sit, the man who has seen the flower maidens, the gilded temptresses of Parsifal the knight. The café, at a diagonal from the Florian, is small and cramped; on the upper floor, a bluish sitting-room, with the calligram of a stairway with a wooden banister. Walking out onto the piazza, on a blustering, drizzly morning, Richard Wagner sees the forest of temptations of the squire never profaned in his quest for the grail – sacred gold for the gold of a body sheathed in dazzling armor. The eyes of Richard

Wagner are cerulean; the forehead is broad; he appears to us as though eternally in profile, unvanquished by age. Richard Wagner walks, amid the pealing of the bells, past the gilded portal of the basilica, crosses the piazza paved in stone, and, making his way toward the velvet luster of the gardens, boards the vaporetto swathed in the somber cotton smoke of a winter morning on the Adriatic, when the water, green and rippled, is a cudgel-blow recoiling from the prow as it embarks.

There are three of them at the railing of the boat's nose, staring into the depths of the lagoon, with its quivers of spectral algae under the wind-racked, turbid downpour. Franz Liszt, Cosima, Richard Wagner, three figures crystallized, dilapidated, indurate, three white aigrettes of hair, forlorn in the saline air. Thus are the tresses of the flower maidens: like the algae lulled and disheveled by the currents in Neptune's lair. On Sundays, a lithe gondola carries Franz Liszt to take Mass in the basilica of San Marco, the *chiesa d'oro*. But now, on the prow of the vessel, the gaunt Magyar abbot with the galvanic eyes and the languid Cosima, nuptially pale, and the man who sees the flower maidens in the forest of the knight's ordeal, perceive the selfsame wind, in the grand aquatic odeum with winged lions.

The paladin will have to avert the lamellate kisses of the flower maidens. Cosima Wagner, in the silky plicatures of Bayreuth, holstered in her widowhood as though in a grey and purple gown, receives, amid the abstraction of limpid waters, the salutations of Mariano Fortuny and Cecilia de Madrazo, some time around the frigid and solitary autumn of 1894, in the aura of the theater, radiant with splendors. The flower maidens are a motionless depression of clarities, fluted and sinuous, beguiling to the touch and to the eyes. Roses in Parsifal's suit of armor. The flower maidens, above all, are floating tresses, frothing in an evanescence gold and reddish in the gaseous light. Color of wild strawberries, feral, with venomous sweetness; eyes closed, as though the naked breast were a carnal eye; tones of vermillion and of copper; the gauze of veils in disarray in a prison tufted in grass. A curtailed storm of colors in languor: the flower maidens in the painting of Mariano Fortuny y Madrazo, in Munich, in the year 1896. Over the green backdrop of a grand Fortuny damask, the canvas faces the casements in the lifeless climate, mute, and unchanging, bathed by the tranquil clarity of the Palazzo Orfei.

The Palazzo Verdramin, final dwelling of Richard Wagner, lies on a silent and abandoned canal; three files of Corinthian columns, their cornices crowned with eagles and coursers, amphoras and roses of stone. Alongside Wagner's lodgings is a pulsing enclosure of tranquil green. The bedroom opens onto a garden with laurels adorned with pink veils and paper roses. They say that in Palermo, when the closets were pulled open, the room where Wagner stayed was overwhelmed by the vertiginous and violent scent of roses. Are roses the flower maidens? Fugacious, they leap from color to color.

All this to take stock of: the canal, the façade, the garden, the laurels, the fleeting shadows of the legions who lived there, the vacant bedroom where Richard Wagner, one cold and sacred February day, died stretched out on a settee, in the palace with the Corinthian frontispiece. To take stock, as well, of this sculpted, kneeling figure of serpentine marble, the white marble of the head and the intertwined hands, anchored to the wall in the atrium. The traveler takes note of it, with rapid strokes, in a notebook he carries in his satchel. In his fretfulness, the traveler recalls a bird of prey: he has, above all, perhaps, the relentless gaze of a bird of prey, under the white hat with the dark band, over the black draft of a moustache and the little beard sharp as a lancet. The traveler who takes note of everything – Gabriele D'Annunzio – may never see the splendor of the flower maidens in the sulfur-lights of the shadowy forest. Yet he still has time to attest to the tulips and roses on a platter. Enough: the hour has come to close the notebook. Gabriele D'Annunzio has a date, amid the damp ochre alleyways and the canals of aurous, lanate green. In the Palazzo Martinengo, Gabriele D'Annunzio must keep his date with Mariano Fortuny y Madrazo, the man who painted the flower maidens.

The Tragedienne

She wears all black. In the depths of the scenery, storm clouds are fraying here and there among the shadows of the starlight. A twisted sapling, on the edge of the wings, exalts the princess martyr, her arms like outstretched wings in the luxuriant and funerary loftiness of her veils. At the tragedienne's feet lies a sallow girl in black, enraptured, eyes closed, a cascade of light brown hair trailing from her sagging head. Under the bobbin lace borders of the tragedienne's squared neckline, a small circular ornament, a medallion, is a bonfire igniting the arms outstretched in bitter lamentation against the storm, the raging sky.

The tragedienne, closing her eyes, lifts her head in the direction of the vast sky. Black hair falls over her shoulders, swathed in a stole; her face is a whiteness laid waste by the immeasurable torture of the spirit's cosmic struggles. Or else the tragedienne may enter, without speaking a word, through a mock arcade on the stage's edge, and pause before a basket of white chrysanthemums resting on the lacquered mahogany lid of a grand piano, and caress the flowers with her hands and afterwards, unhurriedly, sit beside the stucco chimney. Then, from all the stage, we will see nothing more than the brilliance of the tragedienne's hands as she warms herself by the heat of the fire. Eleonora Duse, on the secular inferno of the stage, will be a hand rendered mercy by the benign fire. In the stands, amid a captivated silence, a small man with an anxious bearing breaks into sudden applause at the scene's end; he has the clownlike demeanor of a lunar harlequin and cannot understand Italian. His name is Charles Spencer Chaplin.

It is written: "The mouth kissed me, all atremble." The destiny of Francesca da Rimini is written, in the second circle of Dante's theological hell. In the Palazzo Martinengo, in a room beneath the silken shelter of the solemn and sunlit tapestries, is a small marble bust: an adolescent, his torso encased in an engraved cuirass the color of old ivory, with a dingy patina. A feast for the eyes of Gabriele D'Annunzio, seated among the stretchers for the canvases Fortuny has painted. The tragedienne's destiny is written: the fourth act of *Francesca da Rimini* will be extremely simple, after the sumptuous bombardment of the first three. The piece is motley, barbarous and luxuriant; smoke-clouds of boiling oil in the siege of the castle, and a savage, teeming panoply of figures carved from ancient wood: an astrologer in his conjurer's cap, a minstrel, a Greek slave in the glimmering medieval night. In the fourth act, the sacrificial bell will toll. It is the tragedienne's hour.

"*Amori et dolori sacra*," is written in a notebook with a cover of red leather, which conceals the secret sonnet from a visit to Venice toward the end of September – lacustrine nights, pallid or flagrant in the painted canvas – in the gothic hearth, gilded and marble, of the grand hotel. The tragedienne hears the sudden calling of a voice. We see her in profile: she turns to face Gabriele D'Annunzio, adrift in the corridors of an exquisite sorrow. The destiny of Eleonora Duse is to become, in the words of Gabriele D'Annunzio, in the trappings of gowns and tangible forms afforded by Fortuny, the ill-fated Francesca da Rimini, who receives the trembling kiss of destiny on her spent, sanguineous lips. She stops in the center of the stage. An ancient wind ripples the theater curtains.

At Palazzo Martinengo

The photographic apparatus is generous in scale: a Gilles Frères, eighteen by twenty-four centimeters, purchased in Paris. Mariano Fortuny has a Dubroni stereograph as well, a dark contraption he maneuvers with both hands. On the veranda of the Palazzo Martinengo, Cecilia de Madrazo has paused: a silhouette of shadow – with her spray of hair pulled up in a decorative arrangement like a pagoda – before the broad sheets of glass that rise to the edge of the ceiling. The city is profuse and fragile in the distance, past the parapet on the balcony: a backdrop of blurred houses and the potent premonition of the cupola of San Marco. The veranda lies prone before the darkness and its despotism; on each side, two easels in the gloom, one with a blank canvas, the other, perhaps, with an oil painting. The glare in the glass arcades ordains the monarchy of light beyond the windows.

Mariano Fortuny wears a hat with a tassel emerging from its center. Standing in black shoes on a parquet floor, he poses for a photograph against a backdrop of real and painted flowers. Or in a dark lounge coat, or a doublet, à la seicento, seated in three-quarter profile, against an open window showing a hazy, indistinct landscape, his fingers interwoven, like a figure in a Romantic engraving or a patrician under Titian's paintbrush. All is decoration: a collapsible dome on the ceiling, held aloft by cables, and fringes of tapestries on the smooth surface of the wall, swooning damask on the table and the rocking chair. Luccan ardors.

The camera is ponderous and grand. Of wooden construction, it is held up by a tripod, and moves with Fortuny through the darkness like the shell of a crustacean. Fortuny's eyes gaze through the ground glass. At Palazzo Martinengo, a balcony opens onto the Grand Canal; the fine-drawn tracery in a gothic window's arch is muzzled by the brick wall surrounding it. But standing, Fortuny can lean against the stone parapet and see from the heights a perspective of stalled embarkations in the inert architectural time of a painting by Canaletto. Not long after, they call for him inside: in the hypersensitive emulsion of the photographic plate, the exposure will reveal the seraphic smile of the Princess of Hohenlohe, in an 1830s dress, holding a silver fox in one hand, and in the other, a slender cane with an ivory handle, beneath the august tranquility of a Greek or Roman bust, or in a painting, dreamy against a blurred background of foliage and classical monuments. Turning away from the camera, in a large black hat that erupts into a torrent of flowers, the Princess of Hohenlohe, her hands clothed in white gloves that graze the lace fringe of the sleeves at the elbow, takes a bite, over a plate, of something white, agrarian, and pure, like durum wheat and the nuptial clarity of butter. The white and black of the photographic plate become the white and black of lithographic ink: the lady with the white gloves is a Fortuny *affiche*, for the brand *Tenuta di Sirchiera*.

Villa Pisani

Gabriele D'Annunzio, on the banks of the Brenta, descries a black boat floating downriver. The boat has no navigator: it is being pulled along the bank by two horses with grey coats. In the vicinity of Stra, the river is dark green, the brush on the margins is a tender, luminous green. The sky is white or violet or pinkish beneath the purple splendor of the trees, and their shadows are violet or blue. Gabriele D'Annunzio has left the Venetian daybreak behind. In Venice all the canals were still in the immaculate clarity: deep green water in a bare, pallid light. On terra firma, the morning tram skirts the banks of the Brenta on metallic blue rails. Alongside the current's silver vapor, the tram, painted yellow, passes before the gardens of the deserted villas, the ashen, chafed, discolored stucco, and the solitary statues of nymphs and eighteenth-century gods.

Villa Pisani is utterly alone, its presence amid the lush, dark green of the trees barely suggested by the majesty of the sculptures scattered here and there, or the odd stone dwarf, grotesque, on the outer wall. Then, all at once, one sees the façade. It is not a doll's house, not a bibelot arrayed with ornaments like the painted, varnished carcass of a bureau. It is neither *capriccio* nor *folie* nor *bagatelle*. The morning is now dulcet with sun and the green glimmer of trees; the façade shatters the limpid air with indurate haste, like a colonnaded

21

ship. As he enters, Gabriele D'Annunzio becomes a prince in the villa of princes. Outside, the scorching sun of the Indian summer blesses the dead days with light. On the first landing of the broad, burnished staircase stands the wooden statue of a negro dressed as the exotic stranger in a *fête galante* in a clearing in a chestnut grove by Watteau, or on the grand staircase under the green or gold shimmering foliage of the Villa d'Este, painted by Fragonard in the pellucid twilight. The room of Maximilian, the Archduke, the Emperor of Mexico (*il Messico!* D'Annunzio exclaims), is trimmed in red and fallow, with red satin divans and a chandelier with glass tears. Napoleon's room is completely yellow. Napoleon's bath is a hollow nook, sunken and dark like a pen for livestock: a pit carved in stone with five marble steps leading downward. There is a pale green salon, with portraits of the Austrian duchesses and empresses. Everything seems faded and strangely bare: without dust, without breath, it has the familiar intimacy of death.

From one end to the other are service corridors, and the chambers where the ladies and gentlemen change before attending the balls. They met here: in this room where the figures drawn on the wall feign a bas-relief. They entered the ballroom through the doors of Corinthian bronze with grillwork as delicate as a *trompe l'oeil* painting. The musicians were above, in the gallery where, here and there, Tiepolo painted sundry adornments. Gabriele D'Annunzio and Eleonora Duse are in the center of the enormous ballroom. Through the open balcony, the luster of day is a golden paintbrush that burns without wounding. Looking up, they see, as in the concavity of a ship, the vast apotheosis of the Pisani family in Tiepolo's painting, a serene and solemn set-piece: in perspective, in the open air, an erratic azure of heroes and gods. Destiny of living in the starred darkness, as in the glimmers of a coliseum. In the galleries, the musicians play arias by Cimarosa.

Descending the staircase, the poet and the tragedienne cross regions of petrefact shadow in the shelter of the columns. Pure, the garden: a broad plane of green, sunlit, still with the damp and windblown scent of the rain from the night before. Across the lawn there is a shortcut along the stone edge of the pond to the noble edifice of the stables with its columned vestibule, stern as a Greek temple. But the two lovers prefer to take the paths in the park where the clods of earth, with their odor of rain, and the porous trunks of the trees, coated with moss of a dispirited green, are watched over by the domes of chestnut bowers that plunge down in a delirium of yellow leaves amid the torpor of the autumn morning. The shadows shift with the damp rasping of the leaves. In the distance, beside the colonnade of the stables, stand two towers with spiraling staircases inside and two long paths beneath a vegetal vault of leaves and branches interwoven by some artificer of gardens. It is a sylvan cannonade, with the breath of fragrant rain salving the narrow footpaths. As they leave the trail, heading back, they glimpse a formidable tower: an iron stairway winds around it like a corkscrew, and at the top stands the statue of a solitary soldier. It is the center of the labyrinth.

The labyrinth has a rusted iron gate bordered by two pedestals bearing the Amores mounted on stone dolphins. The labyrinth is a sylvatic geography with avenues of boxwoods: green leaves and yellow leaves in autumnal silence. The time of the statues is the time of the labyrinth; within the boxwoods, within the centuries, in the courtliness swallowed whole by the inky vegetation, greenish and stifling. At the margins of the labyrinth, red roses beneath the nitrous sky. The poet and the tragedienne now hasten their steps, going past the building that houses the stables. A brood of ducks cuts across the teeming yellow firmament. Near the villa itself is another path through the woods, below an eclipsed moon, hallucinated and dramatic under the umbrage of the ancient bowers and the enervating fragrance of the fallen leaves, shining with the gilded clarities of armor. At the end of the path, secluded in the arbor's murk, a solitary statue rises up past a supple, rustic bridge of stone resembling porcelain or Chinese ceramic.

A horse-drawn carriage waits at the Villa Pisani's main entrance. It brings the lovers back to Venice along the banks of the Brenta. With yellow beaks, the ducks splash in the white or silver waters of the river over the flickering reflections of the trees and albid sky. From her dark, diffuse mane, the tragedienne has tied a single hair around each of the poet's fingers. The knots are tender; the knots will have to be broken. The hairs are rent; on each finger snaps a soft, inert manacle. Eleonora Duse shows not even the shadow of a shudder. Nothing can be heard but the fulgent stirring of the water and the thud of the horses' hooves on the mud-caked trail.

Again in Venice, a street; a streetlamp on a corner, emerging from between two cornices on a wall. Wandering, the poet and the tragedienne catch a glimpse, from time to time, of the plebeians' lairs. Under the outstretched fabric of a parasol, the blazing red and totemic green of the fruits from the trees in the orchards. A gentleman passes by in a dark jacket and derby. Two buxom women dressed in black, with broad black kerchiefs over their heads and shoulders, as in the chorus of an ancient tragedy, approach the light of the produce stand. A truculent vagabond from a comedy by Ruzzante or Goldoni rummages through the merchandise, lush and luscious, succulent and solar. In the Villa Pisani's stable, the aphrodisiac, equine stench of the horse grooms rises from the hidden centuries buried beneath the arid stones. On the Venetian street, beneath the snuffed streetlamp, a stocky man with a bundle on his back walks with a rapid step, holding a boy by the hand.

It is only an instant: the boy, in his student cap, stops and turns his head, about to reach his hand out toward the fruit stall, like a capricious Amor in an eighteenth-century garden. Just then, the shutter of Mariano Fortuny's camera snaps the image, grey and white in the trapped incandescence that threads its faltering way across the haze of the photographic plate.

Interlude

Émilienne d'Alençon passes in a victoria along the Avenue du Bois de Boulogne. The thoroughfare is broad; along the pavements walk a woman under an umbrella and two gentlemen conversing in frock coats and top hats, and another man in a derby stands still at the edge of the road, waiting to watch someone like Émilienne d'Alençon pass by. A double current of victorias comes and goes in the ashen distance, with coachmen seated on box seats, the crunch of sawdust, and the creaking of wooden wheels beneath the Paris sky. Émilienne d'Alençon has large golden eyes, and an immense flower-decked hat shadows the oval of her face. At the Universal Exposition in Paris, in the year 1900, James Hillier's Orchestrophone has been presented. It is a large vertical piano, its chiseled wood casing ornamented with volutes and figures of graceful goddesses and musical cupids, their bodies animal and nymphlike as the body of Émilienne d'Alençon: white leggings, cameo face, a strand of pearls wound four times around, adorning a neck the color of wheat. The Orchestrophone, pompous and delapidated, with two pedals and cylindrical molding, gleams destitute before the golden eyes of Émilienne d'Alençon.

Far away, the young Duke of Uzès has died, under an imperious and torrid colonial sun: he had forsaken his teacher's robes for the crinkling shadows in the white petticoats of Émilienne d'Alençon. Smiling from the heights of the victoria at the gentleman at attention on the sidewalk, who doffs his derby to salute her, Émilienne d'Alençon wears the necklace of the Uzès family on her breast: a gift from the frail adolescent from beyond the grave. The victoria, sinuous and silken, has left behind the exhibition's luminaries: along with other carriages, it advances toward the country, the outskirts, medieval and rustic and coarse at first, later softened by a swoon of lather clouds painted by Poussin. They are readying the table in the shadow of the sallows, the weeping willows, the chestnuts, with white tablecloths and dark wooden chairs with wicker bottoms, and bottles of champagne lustrous as the waters of the lake of the dryads, and clinking coupe glasses of clear crystal that shimmer when the sun darts through the calm, translucent foliage. They are all there, behind the table, over the dessert pastries, cloying and baroque: the old satyr, bald and big-bellied, in vest and cravat, and the derelict young man with the torrential black beard and the eyes like a Pre-Raphaelite Christ, and the lady with the nose like a candle douter and owl eyes under her Pamela hat, like a wax figure from the Musée Grevin, and the wag in the panama hat, his mouth twisted in the dismal grimace of a hanged man on some lost corner of the Camino Real, in the boudoirs where pleasure abates like the vigor of dark wine in cask. Émilienne d'Alençon is there as well, radiant, her fingertips frolicking, swathed in piqué leather gloves, under the confectionary pomp of a floral hat. In his panama, Marcel Proust smiles beside her, beneath the benign and aqueous shadow of the trees. The prodigal afternoon squanders itself in radiance.

The Pont Alexandre III is a gilded candelabra, ceremonious on the pillared divan of a velvet and verdigris night on the Seine. Beneath its pontifical dome, the portico of the Petit Palais is flanked by two colossal rows of columns. The rotunda is vast and overwhelms the eyes as you descend from the carriage, still replete with the aquatic light of the river, the gaseous light of the streetlamps, and the silvery light of the stars that adorn the night's taffeta. Coco de Madrazo, whose brushwork scintillates like a young leopard, is tall and slender; he sports a Russian cloak and a black moustache, lets a long head of hair hang free in the tumultuous night of disguises, and masquerades in an Iranian-style tunic. Mimy Franchetti, the errant Venetian in the glare of Paris's ballrooms, wears a white hat with an extravagant crest, and tucks her cheeks beneath the lapels of a mink coat. Liane de Pougy, the courtesan princess, has opted for the classic elegance of a thin ribbon to hold back her hair and a white tulle dress; in the white pliancy of her bosom nests a necklace of pearls wound six times around, with a glimmering cross between her breasts. At nine in the evening, Émilienne d'Alençon makes her entrance in the grand Persian ballroom. She wears a white brocade dress overlaid with gold, and is coated in diamonds, in pearls, in red garnets. Her head is uncovered, the mass of jewels glimmers beneath her tresses. Her hair is stained red with henna, and she inquires whether, by chance, she's shown up late. Marcel Proust, with a slender moustache and a radiant flower in the buttonhole of his waistcoat, smiles at her throughout. Somber in the shadows, there appears another guest to the Persian ball: Mariano Fortuny y Madrazo, in the guise of a Roman *dux*, with a gown of velvet stamped in gold.

Eros's Mirror

Émilienne d'Alençon, her hair colored red, dances the tango in short pants, in the garb of an officer from the navy. For two thousand-franc notes, she has dolled up and beautified a young girl and presented her, on the third Thursday of Lent, to the aged Hennessy. Under the name Liane de Reck, the novice will be on show in Monte Carlo. Émilienne d'Alençon is smoking opium in her sailor's garb, in a bar with ratchet and hurdy-gurdy music. Dark-skinned boys, their faces pale with rice powder, weave together in the submarine shadows of the bar. The scene is turbid and heavy with color, as violent as if seen in the depths of a mirror wet with the foam of a receding tide.

The girl has her back turned; she wears black shoes and thin black stockings that rise to her knees. Her hair, light brown, is gathered in a knot at the nape of her neck. With her very white right hand, she holds the carved wooden frame around a painting of a woman in a melancholy mood; with the other, pressed against the tapestry with Ottoman motifs hanging on the wall, the girl covers her face, which leans slightly leftward and sinks in the suffocating sieve of her hair. Her buttocks are white and limpid like an almond shell before the camera of Mariano Fortuny. In contrast, the dark-skinned girl poses provocatively on a sheet as rife with folds as a curtain in a baroque painting, against a backdrop of tapestries dangling like arms on both sides of a Counter-Reformation chasuble, and displays three concurrent smiles: with Hungarian eyes, with wolfen teeth skirting the heaven of her lips, with the splendor, like a pharaoh's jet-stone scarab, of her starry pubis. Mariano Fortuny's camera is blinded by clarities.

In the murk of the bordello, Sappho and Priapus. The camera of Gabriele D'Annunzio, dark and heavy like a prehistoric beast, films the harried porter with faunlike black hair, carting the silken body of the odalisque. With a ribbon ringing her forehead, the odalisque and the satyr are a single flash of quicksilver on the argentine canvas of the screen, an imprecise image like a copy on carbonized paper, the extremity of its whites and blacks transforming it into an iconic conflagration: the emblem of two bodies. There is tango music in the rooms of the bordello, hoarse like a weary throat, while Gabriele D'Annunzio films the murky salon and the dust-covered alcove, princely and lugubrious.

The Egyptian girl, in profile, has fleshy lips like the pulp of a fruit; her coal-black hair falls in a plait that lays a kiss on her nipple, ravels with the furtive play of her fingers and dies grazing the twin bands of the bracelet circling her arm's supple extension. Nothing but the girl's nakedness, reposing against the darkness behind. Egypt is an abstract notion. In the center of the canvas, painted by John Singer Sargent, the ardent eye reposes on the paired buttocks of the young Egyptian: as she seems to take a step, while her hands move through her hair, their left half, leaden, solar in its tumescence, lies below the hushed bronze luminosity of the right, delicate as a tendril, restrained in heraldic nobility. The axis of the painting falls at the ebon cleft between the two. The Egyptian is the optical obsession of this channel of dark depths in the hearth of her haunches.

In front of a curtain falling with shadowed majesty, the naked woman, her back tense, has one leg folded beneath the other, and her left hand is stroking her hair. In the photographic studio of Mariano Fortuny, the nude model poses facing the darkness of the immense curtain. Her buttocks, in the very center of the frame, are round like a dome or a very clear glass goblet or a clay pitcher roasting in a kiln. We do not see her face. But in this same pose, against the carmine curtain, the buttocks of Velázquez's Venus are nacred pink in color, and her face, in the depths of the mirror, is a nebula that creates, in the spectator's eye, the visible illusion of a face. Henry James, in the National Gallery, takes a few steps back and looks at the pictorial simulacrum in the aqueous, unctuous mirror of the canvas. As he departs the gallery, where the lights are going dim, Trafalgar Square, of a March evening, is a parade of soot lions under a tranquil pale sky soon to sink into a Thames stained the color of lusterless pearl. Not the merest life throbs before the eyes of Henry James.

33

A Visit

Marcel Proust has descended from the gondola alongside the Piazzetta. He comes from the light of the Grand Canal, which traces out a path over the waters, crisscrossing other embarkations like the victorias that cross each other's paths on the slope of the Avenue du Bois de Boulogne. Stepping onto the flagstones, Marcel Proust takes a straight, precise path toward the stone bouquet of the ducal palace. When he reaches the campanile, his path diverges; under the portico, Marcel Proust strolls by the Florian edging past the windows, and arrives at the heart of the piazza's far end, nude as the bronzed body of a slave, gilded and benign beneath a harness of gold in the yoke of the afternoon sun.

Marcel Proust leaves the grand staircase behind him and moves on in a straight line down a narrow street with greyish or reddish walls that cause his steps to echo like the murmur of falling leaves in a forest storm. He arrives at Campo San Moisè: the wrought-iron calligraphy of the railing on the bridge, a diamond of stone over the green diamond of water, and the theatrical tumult of the baroque façade, like the prow of ship in the eye of a hurricane that whips the columns and effigies of saints and ripples the sails and vaults and volutes of the petrified scree in a snowstorm rendered in marble. A snatch of sky, a trembling, tenuous blue: a bright cleft of clouds in the façade's domains, amid a brackish silence, leeching marine light, the color of salt and of orpiment.

After passing over the bridge, Marcel Proust walks right along an alley, more desolate, more shadowy. Angling like the path of a hedge maze, a zigzag brings him to the Teatro la Fenice: a floating altar in the blued crepuscule, its color like the paper of lithographs. Marcel Proust walks beneath a portico, hushed and abysmal like the heart of an Egyptian sarcophagus. Everything is nude and mute stone and bracing, damp light. Marcel Proust turns aside down a street so narrow, two people can hardly pass through it: a glimmer of a glimmer grazes the sunlit fringe foreshortened in the shadowy cavern. Above, three delicate stone arches, whetted by the autumn wind.

Leaving the street, Marcel Proust arrives at a small plaza, exotic and violet, with a Gothic residence. Behind the sharp eye of each of the windows, the shadow of one who lived and died here: Cimarosa, the *musicista* of the filigree arias that resounded in the loggia of the Villa Pisani. The sun shines orange, lashing the lancet windows. Marcel Proust takes the street to his right, and then turns left, astonished at the muteness of the twilight. Passing under another portico, he arrives at the Palazzo Orfei. The façade of the building is in the square of Campo San Beneto, where a well is concealed beneath the ironwork of a pulley that points up to the four balconies and the doubled row of windows. But before he reaches the Campo San Beneto, Marcel Proust enters the main floor of the palace through an open portal in a twilit, confidential street. A deluge of lush ivy, like tarnished bronze, gives succor to his eyes.

On the main floor of the Palazzo Orfei, Mariano Fortuny is wearing a loose tunic, open at the breast like the doublet of a sixteenth-century gentleman. The Palazzo Orfei is the seat of his labors; the Palazzo Orfei is the dwelling of Madame Cecilia. In the subdued, yellowish clarity of the sitting room of the Palazzo Orfei, Cecilia de Madrazo invites Marcel Proust, in the last light of afternoon, to a feast of peaches, succulent and bittersweet, on platters of embossed copper, with a glass of sherry and a dessert of bowtie pastry, the flaky golden dough dusty with powdered sugar. When the afternoon is over and the tablemates no longer see one another, Mariano de Fortuny and Cecilia de Madrazo open, like an inner sanctum, the largest of the chests. In the half-light is a splendor of antique ceremonial garments: one purplish velvet, sanguineous, garnished with pomegranates; another velvet, this time of a dense, dark blue; and brocades and sateens and taffetas and silks, motifs of bouquets or ancient forests that quiver like the wings of a dragon, susurrous, soft, and laminate in the cavernous shadows. Mariano Fortuny, his face turned to Marcel Proust's in the marine, fuliginous twilight, is dressed in a brocade soutane bearing the design of a golden bower.

Latitudes

All the men are attired in hats of grey felt. On the landing of every floor, as we step from the elevator, we hear the metal gonging of typewriters at work. The building is old and capaciously ramshackle: forty floors, in arid darkness, as in an Expressionist film, with walls that look like terra-cotta skin. Up high is a red glow that turns yellow as it strikes the tapering peak of the neighboring structure. The light is warm, as if emerging from the heart of a flaming salamander; or rather, the light's complexion appears warm to the touch of the eyes, of the eyes' sensitive film. Blind, the elevators rise and sink, abandoned in the tremors of the empty skyscraper. When night falls, every window gleams like an icicle; the New York night is electrified beneath the silent detonation of snow. In the nightclubs, the angular tops of the women's dresses expose their backs, and the men wear tuxes, with top hats and bowties. It is the night of the saxophonists. Or better, more vivid, more windblown, it is the night of the theater and the salon and hotel beneath the thick radiance of the fluttering floodlights. The girl from New York sports a Fortuny gown: a slim, pleated dress, its contours snug like the case of a violin, with short, petaline sleeves of silk taffeta and a patterned cotton sash. Over her dress, the girl from New York, in the snowy night of the saxophonists, is wearing a cape: silk chiffon, with florid Kufic motifs overlaying arabesques, festooned with brooches like ice cubes of iridescent glass. The Egyptian sky is concave and free like the billowed sail of an embarkation. In Luxor, amid the Nile's everglade nobility, the skiff slips past like an ancient tumulus. Upright, the Arab in the white djellaba does not show us his face: his gaze is hidden as he stands over the wooden vessel, beneath the harrying of light in the calcareous firmament, in the tempera laid down by Fortuny. Under the calcimine sun, the face of Mariano Fortuny likewise takes shelter beneath the shadow of a felt hat. There is a massif of abrupt angles and an order of columns excavated in the crags, and natives in turbans, their faces dark, in the brilliance of the Bedouin village. Or else, alone, there is Mariano Fortuny, his bamboo cane scrupulous and slight, in the arid absoluteness of the sand, thirsting for lights that quiver in immobile refraction. In midday, in Egypt, it is the desert's Coptic hour. The face of the Sphinx is ever less a face: handbreadth by handbreadth, the bare stone gains ground against her disintegrating features. The face of Mariano Fortuny, in the shadow of his hat brim, blackens and disintegrates like the face of the Sphinx beneath the citrine hammering of the sun.

Ornithology

In a purblind, pulsing darkness, afflicted and secluded like the profaned mummy of an empress, reside the two ladies painted by Carpaccio, with the restless harrier, elegant and airy as a sword, and the cooing, albid dove. The two ladies are swathed in abundant golden dresses: the one above with falcon eyes, the one below with peacock eyes; both with eyes of steel to wound, with eyes of lead to sear, with iron eyes to cleave, with liquid eyes, for they are steeped in the hues of the world in fusion with primordial chaos. The two ladies dressed by Carpaccio, by Hokusai, by Fortuny.

The Traveler

Vienna, is it a box of bonbons? Vienna is a bonbon shop of bubbles. The sky is of gilded, crumpling paper. Every day, at twelve on the dot, the guards in their vermillion tunics, garnished with gleaming gold, enter with their halberds into the emperor's residence. Every day, at one on the dot, beneath the pounding of the gong of the palace clock, the drum major of the palatine band passes through the inner courtyard, leading the changing of the guard: an entourage of soldiers in ceremonial dress, beneath the window of the state room, where the emperor's silhouette is rendered fugitive and hazy in a span of windows lit up by a serpentine sun. The adolescent – Hugo von Hofmannsthal – averts his eyes, clouded over in the candied air. At night, the streets of Vienna are a bar of argentine ice beneath a satin moon. Literature is an affair of gilt-edged books on the table in the salon. Vienna fires a volley of bluish spinning tops.

In Casetta Rossa, the residence of Canova, imperial and shot through with white, a scene is endued with a residue like the veining of purified marble. The Princess of Hohenlohe, with the smile of a Chinese doll, receives the Viennese gentleman, Hugo von Hofmannsthal. In the shadows, in an ornate corner of the salon, Mariano Fortuny and Gabriele D'Annunzio conspire with flamboyant brocades. Herr von N. arrives

43

in Venice from Vienna in the year 1779, at daybreak, in the pink lighted chapel of dawn. Vienna is a theater: décor for the cavalcade, on a white palafren, of a painter disguised in the gown of Peter Paul Rubens. In the harbor in Venice, a company of actors, phantoms, lose their lilac color in the bloodless dawn. Two streets further on, a half-nude gentleman, with a hat and a mask concealing his face, and a ragged jacket, and a blonda lace veil draped over one arm, explains to Herr von N. that the night before, he lost everything at the gaming tables: farobank, presided over by Giacomo Casanova de Seingalt. It now falls to the gentleman in the jacket to drift along the Pescheria, the morning fish market, where the revelers with their florid, incandescent topcoats and the demoiselles with their skin white as eggshell revel in the abalone glow of the breaking day, swallowing bits of scaly fish, salty and triumphal. The night was a table decked with lighted candles, and a sedan chair with a black mask with a nose hooked like a vulture's beak, and a pink smile beneath the painted blue of the plafonds of the palace. Today, on his way to the Piazza San Marco, Herr von N. will see a patrician disguised in a harlequin's garb.

The Venetian September is luminous and confused. The high tide creeps in over the porticoes of San Marco on the side of the Caffè Quadri and reaches the center of the piazza, grazing the patio of the Florian. The people pass in dark attire over rough-hewn wooden planks with bristled edges. Venice is an oceanic palace of gangways. Hugo von Hofmannsthal no longer sees Herr von N., the traveler recently arrived to the Venetian streets. With surly and sublime abruptness, he sees the enigma of Oedipus confronted with the Sphinx, imposing and remote like an inscription in runes. The summer of 1904 desists in an aperture of Adriatic waters when Hugo von

Hofmannsthal, through the portico of the Florian, arrives at the piazzeta, crossed by zigzagging planks that trespass on the water with its reflections of Madrepora coral. The campanile does not exist; it fell, on a July morning, at the very moment of the day when Mariano Fortuny arrived in Venice with a girl named Henriette. In the collapsed clarity of the wreckage is a tumult of scaffolding and pulleys, and foremen at work on the reconstruction. Hugo von Hofmannsthal, walking though the piazzetta in the direction of the quay, sees the skirmish of dragons in the water and the skirmish of bats in the red clouds of autumn. The risen tide, soaking the flagstones, overwhelms the vision of Venice, vast as a diorama. Standing at the aquiline prow of the gondola, Mariano Fortuny captures it with a Kodak Panorama camera. In the image, Hugo von Hofmannsthal will lack a visual existence of his own: the sea, the clouds, and the antique stones admit no peers in the clash in the photographic laboratory.

Embellishment

The non-substance of Vienna? The simulacrum of the state
is the dissolution of the idea of the state in the figure of the
Emperor's person; or rather, in another sense, the dissolution
of the notion of the state, like a capsule, in the choreography
of everyday experience. In the outskirts of Vienna, Hugo von
Hofmannsthal resides in an eighteenth-century palace where
the Viennese spirit has dissolved into embellishments. Elek-
tra leaves the palace once the servants have entered, bearing
amphorae; between the branches of a fig tree, shafts of red
light fall like blotches of blood on the ground and the outer
walls. Clytemnestra, in a scarlet gown, in the company of a
maidservant in a purple dress, rests the weight of her body on
an ivory cane tempestuous with gems. The face of Elektra is
paler than the waxen disc of the moon. The idea of the state
is utterly dissolved, with phosphorescences of silver shading
blue on the blade of Orestes's weapon in the evening of the
palace, oriental and barbaric. Hofmannsthal's Elektra is a
tribal mystery: the arcana of the state reduced to embellish-
ment in the non-substance of the Viennese night.

In the center, an open portico reveals a midground of
very clear blue and a violet backdrop under the pallid moon.
To each side, two skylights and two windows of wrought
iron. A grated bronze door opens onto the apparent void

of a vagabond space wherein, seen from behind, the nude statue of a classical goddess stands upright on a pedestal, the canal between her buttocks in line with the vertical bar of the bronze grillwork in the center of the perspective. To the side, a figure of wounded nobility, clothed in a reddish chlamys with golden folds. The light arrives from this unpeopled lucid space outside, with laurel leaves garnishing the tender, gorged aurora of the naked goddess. Inside – nearer the spectator, on the stage – is a silhouette bent over the handle of a cane, in the tatter of light coming from outside. Closer to the proscenium, still as a figurine, a gentleman in a wig and cassock. The model may be thus, in the bewildering representation of fleeting actions; but perhaps – at the turning point, the interlude, when the conception of the human actions is eluded – the model Fortuny has fashioned for Hugo von Hofmannsthal will be empty and dark, and we will see nothing but the classical goddess in the garden and the noble, wounded figure, whose aspect is likewise statuesque, and the clarity fixed in a motionless gesture that grasps at the chalk-white firmament where the skylights lie. The stage will be a draft of darkness. All of a sudden, it is day: the sky is a spherical surface, concave, opaque white, a screen of colored silk. Not a succession of painted canvases, but a cyclorama of cylinders, the collapsible dome designed by Mariano Fortuny in the Kroll Opera House in the frozen Sanbenito of Berlin. Behind the drawn curtain, the spectators – Mariano Fortuny, Max Reinhardt, Hugo von Hofmannsthal – see, in the adonic white of the theatrical sky, a castle of clouds in contention, with flames laying waste to the space. They are reflections in a painted mirror, projected onto the dome by an oblique source of light, slanted and murky like the insurrection of mottled red surrounding Elektra in the palace of luxuriating death.

Visions

Inert matter bound to living form. Albertine is clothed in a Fortuny dress: with Arabian ornaments, it is dark blue in color, but little by little, as the eyes close in, it changes to fleeting, irresolute gold; the sleeves are lined in the cherry-pink color known as Tiepolo Pink. The vitrines overflow with tunics and gowns: grey in color, mauve in color, festooned with pearls, with Japanese motifs, with lotus flowers, with overlays that recollect the sculpted wood of the old gondolas; heaped on the furnishings, bundled or warm like a stifled storm of gauze and black velvet and silk. The sirocco shifts a cape embossed with gold and silver, with Coptic drawings on the epaulettes and Hellenistic friezes on the roomy shoulders in the trapezoidal night.

Inert matter and living form: Albertine's body, beneath a blue and gold Fortuny dress with pink lining, before the eye of Proust, in the interstices of words, inmate in the banded, rent, and tigrous prison of writing, is a gown in the sumptuous vitrine of words. The flowers evoke the turbans moved by the flaming wind in the light of a Byzantine quay. In the clarity of Paris, in the lampistry of Baghdad, in the bazaar of the nocturnal sky, Marcel Proust, at the forking of words, divines a body below the luminous folds of a Fortuny gown.

Living form for dead matter. As evening falls, Isabella is stretched out on the terrace. The chrysalis of the sun's disc hovers in a sudden, leaden blaze along the margin of the sea; the moon, its color leeched away, attests to the vanishing clouds. All at once, the moon erupts in gold. The gown of the night, extensive in the maritime twilight, takes on the vigor of a palace of torches. Beneath the moon, which looked like a pallid marsh flower and seems now like a canopy of embers, Isabella has draped herself in a design of Fortuny's: an oriental gauze stole with a tinge of pink, like the newborn moon, stamped with a myriad of stars, plants, and beasts. Over a carpet of dark blue and ivory white, Isabella, in bare feet, has heels the color of cinnabar and dances to the jangle of music played on a sistrum. Beyond words, in the realm of paper, Gabriele D'Annunzio watches the barbarous nocturnal dance. Isabella is savage and nude as the scudding of a plane's wings in the raw, uniform sky. The tragedienne has already fled the web of words: Eleonora Duse, utterly alone, a passenger in a gondola as solemn as the bucentaur and august as a Hindustani bark, engages Mariano Fortuny in a colloquy of shadows beneath the wooden ceiling of the Palazzo Orfei, swept by dark murmurs. On the terrace of selenite clarities, Isabella's dance settles in Gabriele D'Annunzio's eyes.

Isabella is transparent like the parchment shade of an oil lamp; Isabella is a Chinese ink figure on a luminous folding screen; and Isabella, if we turn this screen around, is the Marchesa Casati, in the Palazzo Vernier dei Leoni, with the garden's quiet enticements and three broken columns in the clutch of verdant ivy. With lit torches, the black servants stand to her either side, and a Knossos scarf by Fortuny wraps around her, hugging her flesh. On the narrow paths of sundry splendors scattered through the garden, a fearsome fauna of fragrances and beasts: parrots, gorillas, orangutans, serpents, leopards, alaunts, skirting past or whistling or bellowing or swaying in a momentum of confounded color that respires with sultry, savage breath. Gabriele D'Annunzio walks on his toes through the garden with its sylvan aromas. The room is dazzling and red. The girl wears a Fortuny dress of silk taffeta: a Delphos gown, pleated, lilac in color. Her shoulders bare – and stepping, outstretched, in capacious movements through the empty rooms of the Palazzo Barbaro – the girl wears an indigo jacket of silk velvet printed with Moorish motifs in a darker shade of lilac. Her light brown hair is a corsage with resinous glimmers; the girl's nails are painted deep red. She is about to step onto a reddish rug. Before her, to the right, beneath a bouquet of lilies in pale convulsions, the mahogany of Henry James's writing desk is a Havana-colored burst of earthy splendors.

Henriette

Henriette Fortuny is thus, Henriette Fortuny is this: a figure painted in tempera on wood. The frame, on the main floor of the Palazzo Orfei, has a design of gilded flowers. Isolated, the painting, in the illusive and elaborate disorder of the room, reposes before the nudity of a goddess with vegetal adornments housed in a decorative niche in the wall. The portrait of Henriette Fortuny does not touch the wall; it is held up, centrifugal clarity in the ravaged air, by the skeleton of the picture's wooden frame. In the painting, Henriette Fortuny is standing up in the open air; she is wearing a Delphos gown that clings to her body, with a silver Knossos scarf showing a row of darker motifs around her waist and on the borders of the garment. The lining of the gown, the color of wine or pomegranate, projects two feet shod in Greek sandals. The gown's black border covers her cleavage; the spark that spills over her shoulders is the same that inflames the vinous or lilac-colored froth crowning her feet. Henriette Fortuny's hair is blond, she wears gold earrings and gold bangles; a silver veil enshrouds her head and plunges down her back, stamped with motifs in gold and black; a silvery sash, printed with the tunic's dusky flowers, negligently grazes her elbow with its shades of white and gold. The vague eyes of Henriette Fortuny look off toward an invisible distance. *Tu oublieras Henriette,* written with diamond on the window of an inn, was read, on a gelid Geneva dawn, by the gentleman Giacomo Casanova de Seingalt. It was the posthumous present of the departed beloved in the feeble, frozen glow of the Helvetian aurora, when the lacustrine light minted bright coins from the ore of the lackeys' powdered faces. Will we forget Henriette?

Henriette is posed on a bare stone floor that takes on, at the painting's edge, the same decorative character as the motifs on her gown. Behind her, a courtesan garden, of a modulating, diffuse green, with the bases of broken columns, cedes to a frondose forest of green more vibrant in the azure air, and four assegais of cypresses and crags of bronze face the stark blue ray of the sea. The sky is a tempest of blue and green and ash and blackness blotched with light. The leaves of the door are open; the green trembling of the foliage shifts the glimmers on the glass; Henriette Fortuny, standing on the threshold, grasps in her left hand the ample white skirting resembling a bellflower or a bell of lace and tulle, and with her right, she gives a friend a small statue of ivory and wood. Henriette Fortuny's hair is knotted at the nape of her neck, like a sumptuous bruised fruit. Or else Henriette Fortuny is standing utterly alone, against a neutral, whitish backdrop before the steadfast eye of the conjugal camera of Mariano Fortuny: beneath the warm, tender fold of her lips extends the neckline of a yellow dress, while with a hand gloved in white to the elbow, Henriette unfolds, displays, exalts a burnoose of oriental aspect. Or maybe she has left the palace, and we see her on the quay, between the lance of the campanile of San Marco and the stalactite of a noble, nebulous streetlamp and the solemn hook of a gondola: beneath a black hat, with a bamboo cane, in a black dress with two white points, like the sails of a ship or minuscule flames creasing her breast from the depths of her sash. Henriette Fortuny is thus, Henriette Fortuny is this.

The sky, in this oil on canvas, is dissipated and pure; far in the distance loom houses with rustic and archaic roofs. Henriette Fortuny brushes against a stone parapet on a terrace beneath a wind-burst in the open air. Dressed in white, Henriette Fortuny sinks into a shawl assailed and disheveled by the breeze. Henriette Fortuny, under gusts and gales of air, turns her head, raises her shoulders, grasps with one hand the fringe of the shawl around the hollow of her abdomen and her sex with its veil of ceremonial garments. With the other hand at her breast, she struggles to restrain her tresses as they fly from her wind-driven mantle; wind-blown, whispering, like a fluttering fan. Concave and clarion, the celestial vault closes in on the aquiline brilliance of the volleying shawl. Henriette Fortuny is thus, Henriette Fortuny is this.

Nocturne

The vaporization of contemporary time is expressed on an October night in 1926. In her chambers in the grand hotel, Liane de Pougy is bathed in a perfume of carnations. In the cabin on the Lido are cushions, divans, and brocades, and oily furs with haremic glimmers, under pajamas of silk and velvet sewn with golden threads and precious stones. When evening falls, the crowd puts on its makeup in Liane de Pougy's room. A pair of Gitons are dressed as Pierrot; between their lips, each carries a pink rose. Antoine, the coiffeur, is disguised as the Byzantine empress, and his lover as a Chinese Mandarin. They navigate a gondola sent from the home of the Franchettis, where the skies painted by Guardi tremble in vulnerable blue. Upright in the gondola's prow, Coco de Madrazo is crowned with a crest full of feathers. The lantern-lit gondola is flooded with flowers, packed with playing musicians, zigzagging through the waterways, lunary, lunatic, to the Teatro La Fenice, gliding as slight as an ermine cape brushing against the palm of a hand.

Liane de Pougy does not stir from her room; before heading to the theater, a bearded and tuxedoed member of the crowd, disguised as Alfred de Musset, makes a sketch of her reclining in her bed, and like a dusting of carmine, a touch of fever kindles a red glow on the supple skin of her cheeks.

Liane de Pougy, all alone in her chambers, has another theater, another lineage of Venetian love: Mimy Franchetti, with verdant eyes that veer into the color of chestnut, with skin as pale as magnolia and a bluish touch of sky in the shadows of thin veins beneath the flesh of her neck. Mimy was in Deauville, Mimy was in Montparnasse, Mimy is on the stage of memory in the vivid, murky, phosphorescent night in the hotel, when, beneath the row of windows, the fringe of water glistening with moon- and lantern light quivers with the splendor of a Fortuny gown.

The main floor of the Palazzo Orfei is entirely lit up on the evening of the ball: lights with veils of silk and arabesque motifs, or with floral forms, like an inverted, tasseled hat, or in the manner of a chiseled shield, or with strands of pearls and Persian ornaments, or of silk gauze with gilded figures, or, above a table, with feet of rustic forest wood and shades of electroplated metal. Mariano Fortuny, his beard going white, wears a silk velvet cape stamped with gold; Henriette has a part down the center of her hair, cleaving the onyx waves; rings embellish each of her fingers, save for one on each hand, and her shoulders are swathed in a burnoose with seventeenth-century Italianate motifs. Time vaporizes on an October night, time tears and frays in the humid clarities of March. Well into that month, Émilienne d'Alençon covers with roses the free and fickle body and the profaned bedroom of Mimy Franchetti, when all of Paris is a cannonade of glacial winds for the windswept loves with the scent of plucked carnations.

Return to Villa Pisani

The refusal of history is represented by a tapestry, warm and yellow as a lemon, hung from a wooden beam in the Palazzo Orfei. The refusal of history, on the empty quaysides of terra firma, is no longer a golden tramway that passes in the damp, lilaceous morning. The retinues of Adolf Hitler and Benito Mussolini approach along the banks of the Brenta, with that savor of leather and Bakelite in the mouth exuded by the skeletons of the black autos. The light in the villa is imperious and blind, reflecting from the bases of the columns. Napoloeon's bath, built entirely of marble excavated on the grounds of the estate, sinks into funerary silence. At the gate, the autos are a darting black blur like war chariots under the transverberation of the flaming sky. The squeals of the tires unsettle the park with a shrill shred of sound, like the grating of a string on a violin. Benito Mussolini, in Florence four years before, stood in the storm with martial demeanor like the mighty Hercules, sculpted in coarse stone, from a barbarous and remote company of agrarian tightrope walkers; beside him, Adolf Hitler, in a dark and mediocre raincoat, sopping wet with glistening rain, skulked, incensed, like the devil in a marionette theater. Through the row of windows in the Villa Pisani, in the turbulent uprising of 1938, the sky, softened by a centuries-old green, rests, in a glory of dissipated glimmers, on the stony face of Benito Mussolini. A palace is a theater; the stucco represents the dimensions of historic time. On the stairs, sliding past the statue of a black man carved in wood, Adolf Hitler brushes the frenetic dust of carnivorous blackness from his shoulders.

In the chambers of the Archdukes of Austria, in the bedroom of the Corsican usurper, in the ballroom with the triumphant allegory of Tiepolo, in the empty loggias of the courtesan musicians, the man's man and the milksop are engaged in a contra dance of polyhedral clarities. The forested surroundings, irrigated by great rivers and vast floods, have a greener color, of leafy trees, in the atlases of students; the relief of the mountains takes on a tone of tarnished copper in topographic maps of the earth. To mangle green and copper tones, to mangle the tonalities of a revolving planisphere: the phosphoric fusillade fired at Maximilian, in the calcination of Mexico, the ice and stone and hoary treetops of slate in the Tirol, the chocolate décor of the Viennese night. The ballroom is a simulacrum. In a disordered instinct, history is made manifest in the sham of painted walls and empty loggias spinning as on a cyclorama. The thoracic cavity of Benito Mussolini, the exiguous, flaccid, and flagging testicles of Napoleon, the gripping, gluttonous darkness of the licorice of Adolf Hitler's moustache, all enclosed, as in a doll house, in the ballroom with the vanished orchestra, in the white and red brilliance of the patrician walls (History as opera), in the whispering boxwoods (History as labyrinth), in the Greek temple of the stables faced with the fringe of green water of the pond (History as scenography: to simulate History is to make History), walking, with unquiet steps (the larger of the two, a bear; the milksop, a peacock), over narrow, moss-covered paths (History as itinerary, History as garden), under cover of the walls, those grotesque gnomes (History as a puppet play, as a museum of horrors, History as a parade of monsters and dwarves before a savage and sullen god). The sky is scored by a white and yellow flock of ducks. The refusal of history is a Fortuny gown with Coptic designs. Black as crabs, the autos rev with a whine and a burst of gunpowder and give off smoke of quicklime, bitumen, and oil, while the man's man and the milksop, Benito Mussolini and Adolf Hitler, one with a lantern jaw and one with a wisp of moustache, the blackguard in boots and the vizier in slippers, imbibe their liquored and lugubrious libations.

Theaters

When Mariano Fortuny saw it, under a pallid Mussolinian sky, Thespis's wagon was a pointed, heavy sailcloth. Draped in white, in a black hat, Mariano Fortuny entered the scene climbing two steps and pulling the canvas from the frame like a person entering a circus tent. Thespis's wagon, in the ambulatory theatrics of the gleaming fascist autocars, was a diffuse dazzle of dust on the rural roadways. At first, the collapsible dome was nude like an aperçu, an architect's sketch made with a compass in a notebook: curves, tangents, and perpendiculars, an extravagance of steps, structures, and scaffolding supporting a grand opaque cavity. Then, with a hastening of stagehands, the frame drew closed over the concave cavern. When the curtain was raised, the evening spectators, seated in the exit of the village square, see the setting of Orestes: a file of mobile clouds that shift in tone as they pass, now a storm-wracked night, now a tempestuous evening, now, abruptly, a crystalline dawn. A plebeian murmur from the gathered masses before the palace of the Atridae in Argos arrives over the proscenium through the horn of a gramophone. Or another event is commencing – Fortuny, in the wandering theater, perches behind the scenes – and we witness the romantic, romanticized tribulations of the Falconer, with a cypress forest and a lake embraced by verdant vegetation, and the flicker of the fluctuating water with quicksilver margins. When Mariano Fortuny and Benito Mussolini saw it, in July of 1929, in the clarity of a Roman eve, in the clarity of the village dusk, Thespis's wagon glimmered like an idea in transfiguration.

In the time of the narrative, Mariano Fortuny wears a very thick black beard and a white jacket, like a Cossack or a muzhik or an elder from a Russian novel in translation with yellowed covers, for the silver salons and champagne in Paris in 1906: a whiff of stable and an intense perfume of apricots in the nostrils of the despotic Asiatic princes. Mariano Fortuny stands erect before the swooning, luxuriant majesty of the curtain stamped with wreaths of flowers, a solar wheel at its center, like the radiation of a burning star. As the curtain rises in the Comtesse de Béarn's theater, a game of counterlights – the system of indirect lighting patented by Fortuny – reveals, against the vastness of a naked sky, the actresses arrayed in gowns and capes and veils of silk embossed with asymmetric geometrical motifs, in the manner of Cycladic art, as rife with forms as the cloth backdrop is vacant, absorbed in whiteness. The light shifts from red to blue, from yellow to greyish, like the play of reverberations in a magic lantern on the billowing, mobile surfaces of the hanging silks. In the forefront, an actress opens her cape, with a bouquet of flowers in her right hand; the other actresses, with solemn, fragile, hieratic gestures, ascend the ramp in zigzag, setting the veils and flowers to flight, dropping handfuls of flowers from the banisters, with ribbons on their foreheads restraining the jet or gold explosions of their hair. Mariano Fortuny steps back to expose the photographic plate, and the visual field englobes the floor of the proscenium as well as the upper crest of the highest ramp and the dome's deserted zenith. Do not pronounce it

Comtesse de Béarn, but rather Béar; the last letter is silent, an arid luxury, an immemorial secret of writing and pronunciation, transcending custom, like a watchword passed down, immured in the centuries, among the conspirators of some atavistic complot. Marcel Proust did not learn this leafing through the gilt-edged pages of Gotha, but by wresting the remote, terrestrial syllable from the lips of Françoise, the wise servant, ancient and statuesque, like the Venus from a prehistoric tribal grotto. In the time of the narrative, when Mariano Fortuny is exposing the photographic plate, with a lightning burst under the dazzling dome of Thespis's wagon, he is across from Marcel Proust in the florid silk of the theater of the Comtesse de Béarn.

Intermission

Enrico Caruso is seated at the dressing table; face to the mirror, he trims his moustaches with diminutive silver scissors. Enrico Caruso is corpulent, like a swelling vase in a ceramicist's kiln; his hair is dark black, and his face, with its circular opulence, gives prominence to his thick, dark eyebrows, his intense, deep-set eyes, and his redoubtable moustaches, with aglet tips, ascending in filigreed curves: a corkscrew twist of tufted hair with two vertical, pointed extremities. In the mirror, Enrico Caruso watches as Charles Spencer Chaplin enters the room. Caruso does not rise; when they are introduced, he nods his head and carries on trimming his moustaches with fleshy hands. Once finished, he stands and adjusts the buckle of his belt. Caruso resembles an aerostatic balloon; Chaplin is a restless stalk of bamboo. Caruso inclines his ear to the jingling of coins and the rustle of bills that surround Chaplin like the halo of an astral body in the vision of a spiritualist. Chaplin sees Caruso: dressed as a toreador, all silk and gold glimmering with blood, or else in a Huguenot's doublet, with aliferous frills and a white lace collar and satin bands with buttons, or like a libertine prince, all covered in sequins, in the backrooms where lust makes brothers of bodies and sheets in the sultriness of niter. On a pedestal, always: the spherical body is made exultant amid the resonance of a cor anglais and a fiscorn in the center of the theater's acoustical shell. Caruso and Chaplin shake hands on the threshold of the dressing room, just off the side of the stage. He still has time to adjust his clothes before stepping into the scene: he is wearing a short Fortuny cloak, of embossed silk velvet. His collar and cuffs are bright green; the background is whitish, the pattern pale pink dappled or studded with jabs of black or racing green; the silk fabric is the image of a pomegranate flower. At the height of his neck is the blur of a lone black disc. Only for a moment, as Caruso steps away, does Charles Chaplin see, as though magnified, the illuminated stage. The entire theater is aglow with candelabras. Outside, the American night is vast, vaporous, and pink.

The Barcelonan night is fragrant with withered palms on the blind African arcades of the Plaça Reial, and the scent of orange trees in a feudal courtyard in the stone heart of ogees and lancets in the Plaça Sant Jaume. The starscape is a celestial downpour, somnambulant and bluish, on the flagstones flickering under the night's curtain of lapis lazuli. At this hour, when the lights in the shiftless theaters go bright, the clarity is crushed beneath the wrought iron of the Liceu's lanterns. In the Casa de la Ciutat, the staircase falls silent in darkened hollows. The main floor is scored with lashes of gothic light in the archways, and clad in solemn, august vestments of wood and tapestries. The Saló de Cent is stupefied in the silence of centuries lapsed. At that flawless and frozen morning hour, when the sun shines bright like white iron, the hangings arranged by Mariano Fortuny throb amid the clamor of the main floor. With labored efforts, the breath of the night, in the millenary blackness, passes, grazing the cottony, lurid clarity of the damasks.

The Wax Figures

In the Plaça de la Sang, in the peak of winter, 1827. The whole of the ancient, stony village of Reus, pierced by the frigid wind, is a retreat of dried leaves heaped in the heart of the rime. The wind cleans and files the edges of the dwellings. Beneath the violence of the sky, arrested in a condensation of ice, in a numinous fog of clouds, stand four large carts made of rickety, creaking boards. At times, the wind clenches, billowing the folds of the canvas. Standing still in the plaza, scattered by the winter wind, the people are dressed in dark clothes and watch the broken-down carriages depart. The man with the wax figures, beneath the bitter-blowing wind, wraps himself in the coarse fibers of a bristly woolen scarf. He has just finished loading the last of the carriages: all the trappings of a well-furnished house, life-sized, along with its inhabitants. The figures are mannequins; they wear clothes tailored by seamstresses with humming needles, and they have glass eyes, with aqueous globes, embedded in their wax visages. Some are pallid and soft, and some are furibund and wanton: marshals with long sabers, craftsmen clad in ashen garb or in colors strong and vinous. With a fluid, flickering lash of the whip, the man with the wax figures sets his retinue in motion, his wandering museum of statues and tailcoats. The artificer wears a *barretina* of antique, totemic red, like the limp memory of a *pileus*. With an archaic mumble, in a dialect artless, ancestral, and sacred, the country folk refer to him as "Sinyor Marianet, him what makes the statues." Celebrant, they sound out, as if it were a prayer, the august, reverential nickname of the artist in wax, Mariano Fortuny. The line of carriages vanishes on the dusty, sun-furrowed roads, in the parched, conic gusting of the Iberian winds. They stop in Huesca, in the shadows of its prison and monastery; in Segovia, with the luster of its fluid, gilded Alcázar; seven years they spend, eight, on plateaus and mountain ranges, forest canyons and streams that shimmer like mollusk shells, the rumors heard in conches along a seaside of ardent blue, through the charred gateways of inns of slate and soot; they see the rampant eagle on the summit and are deafened by the nocturnal howling of the wolf pack; they exhibit in porticoed plazas where the women, cloaked in black kerchiefs, resemble dusty idols in the heart of an Egyptian pyramid; they exhibit in locations lit with oil lamps and, at the convent of an enclosed order of nuns, they are handed the key to the barren gynaeceum. In the radiance of the garden, the mannequins of wax, with blue helmets and golden buttons, generals' sashes and bands trimmed with gold, ample skirts with august brocades and splendors of alabaster in the cleft between the breasts, wed a theater of courtesan garments with the furious light of the jasmines. The pencil retraces the face of the man with the wax figures. Mariano Fortuny y Marsal has finished the sketch of his grandfather, the artificer of ghosts. The luster of the jasmines is the luster of the vestments concealing the livid bodies, embellished with rouge for a timeworn soiree with theater lamps. In the hands of Mariano Fortuny y Madrazo, the silk velvet, dyed with cochineal red, lets spill a color of jasmine.

Instants

On the 22nd of February, 1920, on the sixth floor of the Théâtre des Champs-Élysées, in the pearlescent cowl of the Parisian sky, Liane de Pougy wears a Ghibelline mantel and a gown of shimmering silver fabric with profuse black designs. On the stage: two clowns dressed in black, or two characters in carnival disguises, hidden behind heads of cardboard. The music is discordant, metallic, discomfiting, with extremes of jangling acoustics. Coco de Madrazo, in the lilaceous snow-drifts of the theater, greets Liane de Pougy. For some time now, on two unfinished canvases, Coco de Madrazo has painted and not painted the face of Liane de Pougy. On the playbills for the Folies Bergère, stuck to the columns on the corners with glimmering glue, with a sweet and sour scent of resinous vapor, Liane de Pougy, her mane unfurled, gazes lost into the erratics, airy heights, her naked feet treading a warrior's helmet and a hunting horn, wound in foliage and water lilies, her body emerging from an exotic web. In the first painting by Coco de Madrazo, Liane de Pougy, the androgyne, is her son, the androgyne Marc – he of the portrait with the Arabian kufiyah and a white fool's cap against a sky strafed by bronze rubble from the sphinx of Giza, on the smoothness of the sand dunes, with the eyes of an emir over a fold of nude lips, the incubated heat of the firmament in which, in the depths of the photo, a lone airplane can be seen. In the first canvas, Liane de Pougy has posed to commemorate the immolated airman with a brushstroke of blurred sky behind the carcass of the airplane. On Coco de Madrazo's second canvas, little more than a sketch, Liane de Pougy is Liane de Pougy herself: in a black hat with white fringes resembling a helmet. Her face is there and not there, composed and decomposed by the pale bleach, the transparent turpentine, pitched against the conspiracy of color.

On June 12, 1894, the sky of Madrid shatters into the blue of a burnished cuirass: a redoubtable sky, without the least trepidation, spilling a vase of blue over the cloudburst of flowers arrayed on the Paseo del Prado. Federico de Madrazo, in an iron coffin, is dressed in a Franciscan habit. Around the grave mound are twelve candelabras and four pedestals with angels, each with seven candles. On the ground, a tapestry coated with flowers shedding their petals, releasing their cloying and discomfiting perfume. The coffin is in the rotunda of the Museo del Prado, beneath the emaciated, abstract theater of Velázquez's Christ in black and ivory, and has, in the shelter of the canopy, the baroque, porcelain innocence of the Immaculate Conception of Murillo. The funeral wreath of the museum's trustees measures two meters in florid diameter. On the 17th of September, 1920, in Paris, all is still sunny and warm, kissing in memory the dead features of Raimundo de Madrazo. Seated impassively at the dressing table, Liane de Pougy, writing a letter of condolence to Coco de Madrazo in the idle luxury of the ramshackle mansion, has at her side a hardbound edition of the works of Victor Hugo and two volumes recounting the life of Christ illustrated with symbolist engravings.

Around July of 1922, in Roscoff, in the rainy regions of Brittany's cliffs, Liane de Pougy wears a peplos of black crêpe and an onyx ring, a coin purse of silvery grey velvet with Chinese ornaments, and a *déshabillé* of mauve crêpe de chine. There is a Brazilian orchestra playing frenetic, aphrodisiac airs, while on the seaside, the wind is violent and the rain assails the castles of the waves. In the labyrinth of Cariocan sounds, amid the white of the cravats and the piano black of the coattails, Coco de Madrazo is quicksilver slipping through the midst of the saxophone blasts, fanning the erotic, feline flame of the mulatto musicians. In Paris, in the clandestine night, soft and defamatory, Reynaldo Hahn has dream-stricken eyes, a small beard, a cane, and gaiters, and walks as though dancing as he emerges with a young ruffian from a dive bar: the Oasis. When they separate, Reynaldo Hahn gives the boy a soft tap on the shoulder with his cane. Wandering, Reynaldo Hahn, eyeing the front windows of the Parisian cafes, meanders like Coco de Madrazo in Roscoff in pursuit of colored saxophonists in the lamplit night, beneath the Lucifer sky. In the glow of the theater balcony, resplendent and rosy, a tenuous, albid light is scattered: the music of Reynaldo Hahn in the Opéra Comique. With deep blue eyes, in the intermission, Marcel Proust arrives, with a ticket from Reynaldo Hahn and Coco de Madrazo for the Princess Liane de Pougy. In the darkness of the balcony, Fortuny's shawls and gowns are creased, rustling radiance.

Around July of 1935, in Le Havre, Liane de Pougy notes down in a blue journal the death of Coco de Madrazo. It is a day enshrouded in a tissue of mist, in a cloaked and febrile spring, on the eve of 1893. Liane de Pougy is consumptive and anemic, and they treat her with the sour, greenish serum of the juice of three bushels of watercress. Liane de Pougy revives; but the tender flesh of her face is dotted with red blotches. Coco de Madrazo kneels down on the steps on the side of the bed and strokes her feet with his warm hands. Gyrating, the two figures, like a gladiola in the bed, are ravaged by a sterile and instantaneous passion. The juvenile spring shatters on the windows of the mortuary summer.

The Lovers

At evening, a man beaten down by the years, with a white beard and black coat and a hat with a white brim and dark crown, deserts the verdant light, which seems filtered through bottle glass, of the rooms at the Palazzo Orfei. In the wind-swept crest of autumn, the palaces and churches and tottering dwellings of Venice are fragments of a stone ornament hewn with tremulous mists, like the crags of Montserrat when they visit them at daybreak one sunny, nuptial June, Mariano Fortuny y Marsal and Cecilia de Madrazo, in the clerical, chromatic clarity of 1868, or the peaks of Montserrat when, fleeing the spell of the flower maidens, the paladin Parsifal arrives at the sacred secret. Venice is sodden with tides, a liquid gauze of fog over gauze battlements of stone and gemstone; Venice is a dark sky that rumbles and reverberates like the curved carcass of a ship. Mariano Fortuny y Madrazo, on the road running alongside Casa Cimarosa, holding Henriette by the arm, in the vigor of the cool autumn air, is a lone impulse of wounded clarity. The seats of the Teatro La Fenice are upholstered in velvet; in very back of the grand balcony in the center are suspended vermillion damasks with their majesty of destitute tassels and fringes. The roof is of a pallid green with green and pink figures painted in fresco; the crystal chandelier has a very white glimmer; the balconies are burnished with a

PERE GIMFERRER

trilling, liquid saffron light. As the curtain rises, Mariano
Fortuny sees, half-hidden by a large tapestry, the deck of the
ship that takes the lovers from Ireland to Cornwall.

Around 1900, Mariano Fortuny, in a Moor's djellaba or
the toga of a *dux* festooned with pennants, saw the deck of
Tristan's ship, the mast and the bridge of the stern deck and
the canopy that encloses Isolde's bed before the grandiose
splendor of the sea. Mariano Fortuny's model for the Teatro
alla Scalla takes us on board, to the canopy: opposite the dif-
fuse, rocky distance, a panoply of sails in the shelter of the
intersecting masts and spars, and a castle of braces under the
vault that ends in a sharp peak of dark sails. In the middle,
a lone figure, with a tunic of abundant folds, observes the
blue hems of the sea and the hint of green escarpments on
the expanses of Cornwall. In La Fenice, the music, dissolved
in aquatic, nocturnal clarities, trembles like a living gem in
the dark heart of the Venetian night. Tristan and Isolde are
a quickening, higher, deeper, darker, that impels them and
makes of them a single current in the sluices of time: violated,
violent, and inviolate. Against a backdrop draped in a Fortuny
tapestry, with an unfurling of ducal flowers, the two figures
become visible over a pedestal. They are nude chiaroscuro
forms, with one foot planted on the ground and the other in
a reticent dance, two thrusts of powerful haunches and of
burning, furtive bellies, with the arboresque, wooden hard-
ness of sex, and arms wrapped around torsos, and their hair
like petrified carbon, volcanic black glass: detained in the
moment consecrated by fusion, at the fore of the ornamented
drapery, the lovers are a Fortuny bronze. Or, beneath the pas-
sional and vigorous wind-burst rifling through the tree leaves
and billowing his tempestuous hair, the Wagnerian warrior,
cloaked in a cape, has the blade of his sword swathed in the

sash that falls from the gown of the Valkyrie, undone by a gust of air. The woman's nude shoulders, pressed into the man's body, have a luster as live as the foliage in the light, paradisiac and infernal, of Fortuny's painted canvas.

Departing from the theater, the cream clarity of the streetlamps has illumined, in the deserted sky, the white bouquet of the moon.

The Sphinx

Madame du Barry steps down from a carriage with orna-
mented wood on the radials of its wheels. Madame du Barry
carries an open umbrella of white gauze: against the carriage
door, the parasol's whiteness jousts with the whiteness of the
undulant, quivering feathers on the wide-brimmed picture
hat and the lather of lace that garnishes her sleeves and shields
her cleavage. The carriage frame is a fretful festooned frog:
Madame du Barry dissipates in the soapy suavity of her pan-
nier. But the eye, upon seeing her, is forced to rest in three
places: on the fist of her right hand, closed like a gauntlet over
the umbrella's nacred handle; on the soft, tempered explosion
of her left hand, resting on her waist, with ringed clarities on
the corolla of the crinoline; on the solar brilliance of her black
hair and her obsidian Aztec features. Dolores del Río, on the
Warner set, is an enclosure of precipitous light. A black hood
of hair hugs her head; on each side of her face, beneath the
platinum scallops of her pendant earrings, her black dress
gives way to two barbed vampire's wings; on the blackness
of her breast, the sole glimmers shine from a large brooch of
gemstones with a pure pearl in the heart of the circle. Dolores
del Río looks up; beneath the bent and somber streak of her
brows, over the lake of her iris, her black pupils, throbbing
fluently between the butterfly flutter of her eyelashes, are

79

consumed in a condensation of flickers, very far from the freckle adorning her cheek and her archaic, Hottentot nostrils and the obsessive blur of her lips rendered chocolate with a bright, thickened pigment. Or Dolores del Río, against the white screen of closed shutters in the background, marries the darkness of her skin, of a tarnished copper idol, with the absolute black of a shawl with elytron wings and the albid plummet of her dress. Blinded amid whiteness and blackness, Dolores del Río no longer looks up; she looks straight ahead, to the place where that unseen, unseeable form is emerging, projecting a broken, angular shadow, cutting like a guillotine the partition between the two wings of the shutters. Her eyes are alight, expectant, and mystic. She looks at us.

Dolores del Río, not far from Mexico, inspissate like syrup beneath the distilled sun, smiles like a fetish in the salon: lustrous frock-coats, gilded uniforms, necklines the color of broom, in a world that is a small silver box. Dolores del Río, beyond the satin décor of the carriages, in a focal, centrifugal light, lives, in the clarity of California, in a white house with round windows with iron bars and wood columns with baldachin majesties and willows entwined with ivy and mosaics arranged like a chessboard. Outside, the California night is restive, firm, obsessive, and burned; and yet, if you press a button on the wall, you will set in motion an ingenious mechanism that lets loose, to remedy the nostalgia of the acrid, absolute earth, an artificial downpour, smothering the windows with a tropical curtain of rain-swept light.

On the set, Orson Welles is in a Russian coat, swathed in the fur of Hyrcanian beasts, like the Slavic overcoat of Coco de Madrazo in the soirees at the Petit Palais. The assortment is powerful and plumed, phosphoric and bosphoric amid the glimmers of the Bosphorus. In the Turkish night of turquoise,

the downpour, violent and white in the blackened light, flat-
tens the bare curtain, glances the brim of the hat, fogs up
the glasses of the assassin in Istanbul. The deck of the ship
is timbered and Balkan under the tragic clouds in dissolu-
tion. The camera blackens on the tripod's peak. Through the
camera's eye, on the deserted, torrid set reigned over by the
eye of Orson Welles, Dolores del Río, in the mocha night
of the Ottoman cabaret, cloaks herself, by the tables with
their lamé coverings and champagne glasses, in a tiger's pelt
cinched around the waist. The number onstage in the Mus-
lim café, in the dance hall, depicts two felines in heat: the
man is a boorish barbarian, with a tufted torso and lustrous,
pomaded hair; Dolores del Río, her thighs sheathed in dark
fishnet, pulls the pelt tight over her naked body and nestles
in a hood of tigrine pillage, crowned with the beast's ears and
whiskers. The tiger's mouth is agape: from the cavern of its
throat, the face of Dolores del Río is born, in the cameo of the
savage hide. In Xanadu's park, the wild beasts catch a whiff
of the master of the house's death. Dolores del Río, in a white
flounced skirt with black trim, may dance with Fred Astaire
in his black tuxedo and a white carnation in his buttonhole.
In the night's Turkish cabaret, in a tiger's skin, or on the set of
Xanadu, Dolores del Río, colonial remnant of exotic empires,
is a sphinx beside the deadpan shadow of Orson Welles. They
are two destinies; they are party to destiny. Under a white
stucco column with a Doric capital, a spotlight falls on the
floor, and two more rise up to the tips of metal bars over the
head of Dolores del Río. It comes from the Malibu beaches,
this murderous cushion of air; it comes from Malibu. The stu-
dio photographer raises his arm, giving the signal. Dolores del
Río stretches her arms out from her torso, the fingers of each
hand splayed and splendid with rings, her body close to the

torn backdrop. Her hair, formerly parted down the middle, is now a smooth helmet of intangible black. Dolores del Río, at the zenith of the year 1941, is wearing a Fortuny Delphos gown with a ribbon wrapped around her waist, and the fold of a pleated, ornate edge, cut out in the form of a heart, hints at the columnar darkness of her groin. Her left hand, tentative, hangs in the virgin void of silver and alabaster.

Encounters

In the spring of 1921, in the verdigris of Paris's air, Georges Simenon resides in the Place des Vosges. The square is imperial and ocher, nestled in the peaks of the roofs as in the folds of rubicund tunics. Beneath the arcades, toward the Rue du Pas-de-la-Mule, the stropping medieval wind hones the stone knives of the arches. Balas in color, brighter than ruby, the same shade as red earthenware, the houses are ferruginous puncheons. In the whirlwind of Paris, a gust of white specks in the paper cone of the February sky. La Vendée is fierce, fanatical, and blinded; the Château de Terre-Neuve, in Fontenay-le-Comte, in the heart of the soured speck of land, unfolds in barbed towers in the glowing garnets of winter. The steps in the Place des Vosges resound in the matte luminosity. In the courtyard of the château in Fonteney-le-Comte, beneath the towers' thronged spurs, Georges Simenon trims the trees of the garden with large, glimmering scissors. He wears a floppy hat with a bobbing brim; a hat of the kind you hollow out in the crown with the palm of your hand, running it around the inside of the rim, the sweet spot where it falls onto the skin.

Henry Miller, simian in aspect, in the fur-lined grey of the Clichy days, is wearing a wrinkled suit and walking with rapid, nervous steps. Henry Miller is in the heart of Big Sur, sumptuous and deep, like the pulp of a pomegranate burst

83

apart with a single fist-blow, precise as the palm skirting the brim of Georges Simenon's hat. From the height of the Ponte dell'Accademia, in the verdant, emerald clarity of the Venetian September, the sun darts over the terrace of the ogival hotel where Georges Simenon has sat down to write. The light ricochets off the round lenses of his spectacles. In the outskirts of Lausanne, Lake Geneva is sugared and shimmering like an aquamarine. On the grass-lined roadways, in the morning, yellow buses, blue trolleys, and bicycles of silvery chrome glide by. Charles Spencer Chaplin, at the edge of Lake Geneva, is wearing shorts and a white polo shirt with black dots. Charles Spencer Chaplin, with white hair, tries out a few dance steps with Geraldine Chaplin beneath the bright light on the set. Henry Miller, faunlike and dancerly, arrives through the garden; Georges Simenon, opaque, has a round tin of pipe tobacco on the table. Henry Miller, Georges Simenon, and Charles Spencer Chaplin, in the fiefdom of the regions of Lausanne, in the aperture of light in the estate, are seated at a round table after dining. The three rest their heads on the palms of their hands, their elbows ensconced like jewels in their settings, almost touching, and they look at one another, and the night passes by while they laugh and cry. Diamonds.

Oona Chaplin, her hair gathered on the nape of her neck and parted down the middle, is wearing a silk veil and a Fortuny Delphos gown that stretches down to her feet. The terrace is kindled with mineral light beneath the roasted unfurling of the Castilian sky. The greenery clutches at the balustrade with its delirium of cornices. On the line of the horizon, above the columns of the parapet, the Castilian forest is an intensity of holly oaks. The edge of the Fortuny Delphos gown reaches the ankles of Oona Chaplin, who kisses the ground with her bare feet, and as her eyelids descend like a Polynesian goddess's, she opens her arms wide and lets float the foam of her veil in the broad sky, rife with wind-wracked ardor. The Fortuny patterns, in the sendal made bristly by the aerial light, are motifs of aquatic flowers, like the flickering floor of the green and blue sea.

Episode

Valentino is a vain vauntmure, a vane of vanilla in veils. Rudolph Valentino, in the studio's elevator, gazes into an Irish boy's emerald eyes. The hands touch; only the fingertips. At four in the morning, Paris is nude: on the Boulevard des Italiens, Valentino sees the face of Valentino on a poster that the wind frays to ribbons in the porcelain light. The Opéra, in the fishbowl of morning, is a cascading coiffure corrupted in petrified gold. Valentino walks through the empty streets beneath a moon of silk. The door to the street opens and closes again quickly; as it does, Valentino and the French boy kiss on the stairway. The bodies, in the aube, have a tiger-like shimmer. Valentino's car is upholstered in leopard skin. In the couples' suite in the hotel, Natacha Rambova rejects the scuffing of Valentino's humid, febrile body. Light of virgin vauntmures. Valentino in vestments of white and gold. Valentino slicks back his hair with black pomade. Valentino wears a white robe with a gilded dragon on the breast. Valentino embraces the lady of the camellias. He is dressed all in black, with the gold chain of a pocket watch hanging from his belt. His hair glimmers with brushed and brilliantined light. The lady of the camellias lets her head loll back, like a dark waterfall grazing her argentine fox stole. The lady of the camellias is Alla Nazimova. Rudolph Valentino and Natacha

87

Rambova are dancing a tango. He is dressed as a cowboy, with very shiny black boots. She wears a black skirt, tight on her haunches, that billows with the clarity of curtains down to its tasseled edge.

Alla Nazimova is standing, spirited, between the twinned glimmer of two lamps, in the vaporous, velvet chiaroscuro of the bedroom. Her eyes are two Chinese fish. The Fortuny Delphos gown robes her silvered stomach and her liturgical breasts in light. The long Fortuny coat is made of velvet, with drawings of eyes whose forms are at once solar and floral. Natacha Rambova is standing, in the photographic daybreak, in the center of the nude room. An alcove of buffeted soap-bubble clouds for the lovers' bodies: Natacha Rambova and Alla Nazimova, the pup and the she-wolf, kissing in the melee of linen, rending the lagoonal canvas of light, like the warmth of sealskin on shoulders of gold in the bare-breasted night. Natacha Rambova dissolves into delicacy. Natacha Rambova sees the astral body of Valentino with the clarity of a spiritualist's aura. Natacha Rambova wears a silver diadem on her head and has come to rest like a Hindu dancer trapped in the daze of angular lights that rip and pierce the folds of the Fortuny Delphos gown. Valentino is a violin.

Sisterly

The man in the straw hat – the man in the white panama hat – is standing next to the platform. Eleven steps of sylvan wood lead to the guillotine's edge. In the broad plaza with its wheaten light, the people rush to the windows as if moved by a mechanical spring. On the streets of Paris, cobbled and mute, gallops Danton's horse. The plebes, in chorus, espy the brilliance of blued steel on the guillotine's blade, lucid and sharp like the air of the Parisian morning. David Wark Griffith, the cinema director, crowned in a panama hat, makes a sign with his left hand from the platform. The hooves of Danton's horse strike sparks from the Parisian flagstones with the scent of an herbarium or the stench of muck. Bluish embers on the street, bluish embers on the guillotine. Paris is a stage.

The two sisters are seated, facing one another, in the French room. They are dressed in exactly the same sort of pleated hat, like a creased, crumpled Sanbenito, and have the same hair, black and disarrayed. To the left, Lillian Gish, seated in a wooden chair with a slatted backrest, is sewing a delicate linen; to the right, Dorothy Gish, sunken in a small armchair, leaves an embroidered blanket with floral motifs resting on the edge of her seat, abandons her hands on her pale skirt, and fixes her eyes on something on the back wall of the room, something not visible. Visible is the visive vertigo of the immense mirrors that hang from the ceiling. The light detonates the mirrors' fluid interior; the light, pliable, wounds a fine veil of winnowing gauze extended over the spectacle of Lillian Gish's head in the drunken, thirsting leech of the spotlight's glare. Dorothy Gish is seated in the back, wearing a long Fortuny Delphos gown with sleeves that hang as smooth and hard as laminated silver. Over her arms there falls mechanically, halting as it touches the elbow, a Fortuny jacket of silk velvet. The light is concentrated on the patch of empty wall, behind the splendor of Dorothy Gish's black head of hair. In the foreground, the portrait painter, with his back turned, has a half-finished oil painting on his easel. The hands are still a pastel smudge; the face, which in nature is a chocolate tablet of coquetry, becomes the rugose pucker of a witch's gargoyle in the painting. One eye is unfinished and still lacks a pupil.

The first thing we see is a screen of white gauze wounded by the pallid outpouring of light. On its underside, the clarity carves out the right angle, sharp and stern, of a dressing table; above, the erring eye is lost in the undulation of vegetal delicacies on a curtain overrun by sinuosity. In the background, in the darkness, an inlaid wooden door. The body of a girl is a vase, narrow at the feet and undulate from the ankles to the waist, smooth as a frothing champagne bottle. The girl emerges from behind a folding screen with a wooden frame lined with spotted velvet. With her fingertips she cinches softly, in the hollow of her shoulder, the neck of the long Fortuny Delphos gown. The face of the girl – Lillian Gish – is naked and precise like the flesh of the Venus in the mirror. Nudity is transparent. Nudity is a transparency. It is transparent. It is a transparency. It is transparency.

Table Talk

The sky is of an intense and very fulgid blue; the light falls like lead, straight downward, at the burning point of two in the afternoon. The blue brilliance of the sky is piquant; it filters through the fine taffeta sieve like the mask of a dark green garden concealing a terrace where a meal is to be served. The blue clarity of the sky is impenetrable as a suit of armor. A trellis of roses twines up toward the terrace; a black sheet, its border the ochre of old gold, hangs from the lattice, grazing the roses. The blue of the sky is beating like a heart. The wall supporting the balcony is rubble-white, affronted by the clarity; here and there the cement chips away and we can see the red of the bricks. At the edge of the wall lives the green grass of the hill of the Alhambra. Andalusian glimmers, glimmers of Boabdil. The white of the wall is strong, and abounds with light. In the center of the meadow is a pink cluster of roses.

The lady, seated on a stone bench in the meadow, has a coiled bun of hair on the nape of her neck. Her skirt is white satin with nacred reflections, their light as alive as the white-washed wall. In a fold in her skirt is a rent of red shadow; if we squint our eye and move back a few steps, it takes on a shading of black. The lady is clothed in a carmine shawl, with blotches of yellow and blue and green, and a vermillion veil adorned with a rose, and holds in her hand a collapsible fan with cloth overlaying its slats. Laid out in the meadow is a man in country dress, plucking a mandolin; between his feet, a red cloth lies over the ground, the lining of his coat, perhaps. Not far from the man's head, the flush of two oranges; spherical, very close, only one of them still glimmers. Next to the lady, a man in a blue-grey three-piece suit and a hat of soft felt, smoking a Havana cigar, sits up straight, causing his seat to tip as he remarks on the game of Spanish cards contested on the small table in the meadow. A man standing up, rustically quixotic and conceited, wears a red sash and a leather hat, after the fashion of sheepherders; another one, seated, also wears a red sash, wrapped around his waist. The card game is their affair. Flush with the table, panting, the brick-red, fleeting tongue of a dog darts in and out. Above the wall, beyond the wall, yellowish masses of dry weeds and underbrush; up high, atop the parapet on the balcony, a pot of geraniums.

It is Granada, in the summer of 1872. Next to the geraniums, the gaze lights on the heads of two children. The girl, with black hair, looks at the boy; the boy, his hair golden, watches the goings-on. We see his head in profile, turning downward. "It's me." In the oil on canvas painted by Mariano Fortuny y Marsal, Mariano Fortuny y Madrazo sees himself in the light of Granada, on the hillside of the Alhambra, over the tabletop of chalk-white, red, and gold: nothing but a shimmer of golden hair on the head of a stripling in the violent light. Mariano Fortuny y Madrazo signs the letter with a flourish. We are in Venice, on the 8th of January, 1949, when the whole of the sky is mist and gauze.

Portrait

Mariano Fortuny y Madrazo is tall like a tsar in the sylvan rooms with Slavic glints in the Palazzo Orfei. When the wind-bursts storm the yellow streets, or when the summer's pincers prick the green waters, Mariano Fortuny y Madrazo's dress is unchanged: a white silk tie, a short cape of black linen, a black hat, low-heeled shoes of cordovan leather or red sandals. His hands are in his pockets; when he listens, when he speaks, his lips describe a half-smile, but the depths of his face remain closed and impassive. Mariano Fortuny y Madrazo was a heap of gold snow set afire on the wall in Granada; Mariano Fortuny y Madrazo, in 1880, wears short pants and gaiters and takes shelter against a wall, so as not to be swept up by the wind-burst of Paris's light. Below the part in his hair, there is something in his eyes that refuses to give itself over entirely. No. Mariano Fortuny y Madrazo stands in profile, sometime in 1922, with his hair disheveled and his shirt open at the breast, a fold of whitish kerchief in his right hand rendered lamellate by the brilliance of the light. His left hand nestles in the pocket of his cloak; his beard is noble, substantial, and black; his eyes, just shy of a squint, look neither ahead nor upward: staring downward, they liquefy in dreams. Venice is a trumpet of green-blue light in a sodden street. With the electrified smock of a Faustian lampist at the quivering trusses of the cables, Mariano Fortuny y Madrazo appears in negative: a beard with eyes turning inward, turning downward, untroubled by the vision of the visible. Needles, amperes in the hum of the spotlights.

Face to face: Mariano Fortuny has a white beard and looks at himself, painting on an easel attached to a mobile chair that glides back and forth on a set of tracks. The brushes are fine and firm like his flamboyant eyes. The eyes look directly into the eyes of Mariano Fortuny y Madrazo, in the optical bombardment of the studio, in the clarity of 1930. Enfeebled, toward 1947, Mariano Fortuny y Madrazo is a burst of white hairs and eyelashes and whiskers and beard laying waste to a furrow-wracked pallor. The eyes are firm with steely blue like the Moorish sky over the Alhambra. Granada is a stony summit with towers, a welcoming plain, a horizon of hilltops and azure crags stretched out before Mariano Fortuny's bedroom. Granada is an arrangement of lights by Fortuny.

We see him in the courtyard of Castello Sforzesco, askance, some time in 1937. The actors are clad in plush seventeenth-century garments touched with gold. The light is a red raptor the color of dark iron, prowling through the bright sky of Milan. Next to the woman in the bicorne hat and pleated skirt, lighting her cigarette, next to the gentleman with his head uncovered, in a mantel and cape with floral motifs, his hair slicked down with brilliantine, Mariano Fortuny y Madrazo turns in his black hat: only his face, in three-quarter profile, saying something to one of the stagehands. The lenses of the glasses of Mariano Fortuny are a round dazzle of white. Askance, face to face: something forever remains closed. The eye denies to the eye the vision in the eye's depths.

The Business

Fortuny is a fabricant and a factory with a patent. Fortuny is a firm in filigree. *Fortuny-Venise*: glossy black letters on the gold silk disc of a tag marring a fabric of blue velvet. *Fortuny-Knossos*: Hellenic letters, archaic around a Cretan drawing of a labyrinth. *Société Anonyme Fortuny Venise*: corkscrew motifs resembling a dragonfly, damselfly, eye, or flowers in fifteenth-century patterns. *Direction Bureaux 805 Giudecca*: the girls, with paintbrushes in their hands, retouch a sheet of printed cotton. The girls are at work, one standing, with a white blouse corralled in a fading halo of pale light; the other is seated in the dark deluge of dead glimmers on a wooden bench, mending the hem of a lustrous cloth. They have no face. Henriette has no face in the diapositive, painting on a printing plate while the light drinks her down. *Fortuny Inc.*: in the grand hotel, a spur like a spiritual state in the blue sea, *poolside suites decorated with Fortuny fabrics*. The printing press, under sheaves of iron and metal screens, has casters and cylinders and shoots out sheets of fabric in silken shivers.

The business is here: the prohibition barring importation of silk from Japan, the embargo on silk and velvet, the authorization to import silk (but not velvet), cotton velvet instead of silk velvet, excesses and scarcities in the baccarat of bankruptcy, the closing of the factory at the height of the blockade, Mariano Fortuny y Madrazo, painting in an Arabian tent mounted in the grand salon of the Palazzo Orfei, while outside, the damp and saline wind scatters the cotton-weave texture of the clouds in the Venetian sky. Expansive, the business ebbs and flows. In the center, the pattern of a gown of silk gauze and a velvet dress with borders of flowers in vases and fountains of youth.

The Dwelling

There is the head of a bull, white like the sun-bitten sand. A real bull's head, like a tribal trophy. Antique colors of knives and nudes and capes. The room is put in order: the order of the materials, on the main floor of the Palazzo Orfei, is marked by an obsessive *horror vacui*. Not a single gap: like one who would polish words with hard diamonds and flintstone, and populate each page, each line until the complete emptiness becomes an empty completeness. Nothing divides the room but hanging tapestries. Brushing past each one, from one side to the other, Mariano Fortuny proceeds, his breath stifled by brocades. The seated lady, in the copy of Tiepolo, has a face of white ceramic and a tumultuous blue mantle. At the entrance, the right side of the room has false friezes of frondose, Edenic antiquity beneath the clarion whiteness of the bull's skull. To the left, the room explodes: the path of Mariano Fortuny y Madrazo, after taking a turn around the large wood table, under the aqueous eye of the flower maidens and the brambly beard of the painted prelate with the reddish gown, flees the pearled clarity of the windows and plunges, beyond the tapestries, into the Moorish opacity. Opposite the closed balcony – a sieve, an Aida cloth for the silken light – the grand wooden staircase, in the heart of the main floor, has thirty steps, and a landing as well. Mariano Fortuny stands at a vantage point at the head of the stairs, like a Caliph commanding his maritime empire of palafitte palaces in the Red Sea. Further back, Mariano Fortuny y Madrazo, with a whisper of sandals of cordovan leather shuffling beneath the roof, in the darkness, florid as a cameo, arrives at the explosion, behind a pane of glass, of the flaking tempestuous hair of the bust of Mariano Fortuny.

The day is inexistent. The Lumière Autochromes lend a muted, silky tone. The young model, standing in profile before a backdrop of forests painted on canvas, with leafy, ephemeral trunks, has ash-blond hair and smiles faintly, with a touch of blush in the momentary dimple in her cheek and blood rising in her neck, delicate as the toasting of a crystal glass and a rose trapped in a cleft between fingers beside a gold ring. Over her shoulders falls a large velvet cape, resembling an Arabian burnoose, its ornaments derived from Tuscan motifs from 1600. All is black and gold, flickering in the eyes, on the pallid green of a floor cushion and the carmine of the tapestry that embraces the invisible columbine whiteness of her feet. No color is too insistent in the Lumière Autochromes: dark green and mauve and light green and ivory and lilac; ash-grey and garnet and cool pink and hot, forceful in a tide of unfurled cloths in the main floor of the Palazzo Orfei. Mariano Fortuny y Madrazo turns: on the white background of the canvas, beside the bull's two horns, he has painted a death mask. The white of the bull: the color of death. The garnet and carmine are defiant in the face of the amber and emerald green of the seaside daytime in Venice. There is no time, no death in the time of the tapestries of the Palazzo Orfei.

The Resolution

The carnival mask is inverted. The carnival mask is adorned with a crest of white feathers, its color is greenish bronze, gemstones surround the oval of its face, and there are two holes to be looked through by the eyes of the girl who carries the mask in her hand. The mask is nocturnal; in the Piazza San Marco, in the fullness of the sun, of soft, molten gold, the mask falls into a fold in the velvet cape. The column at the basilica's entrance is daubed with gold as ancient as the leathercraft reflections in the gothic filaments of the ducal palace's porticoes. Beneath a Fortuny cowl, with a Fortuny cape, Julie Christie has a carnival mask in her hand and is looking at the center of the empty square, her hair blond as the column and the sun-shimmer that chisels the folds of her profile in gold. In the Muslim and medieval cavern of the Palazzo Orfei, Julie Christie is wearing a rumpled gown of sanguineous silk beneath the shelter of an Asiatic warrior's helmet, and Fortuny breeches of rumpled green silk that cling to the medusa of her pubis. Above the mace and the shield and the coarse halter from the armory of the salon, the summer sun of 1973 yellows the crest of the fallen carnival mask.

The entry to the Exhibition, in Barcelona in 1929, mimics the form and red color of the campanile of the Piazza San Marco. Festive fountains, decorative mountains, and beyond them, simulacra: a Rome without Bramante, the tower-capped fiefdom, incastled and Tuareg, of the fortifications of Avila, mosaic and chessboards of glazed Spanish tiles, the condensation of pictorial space in the visual space of imitation: Spain as Morisco ornament. Along the paths, the lighted waters grow drunk on blue and supple green. On the summit of Montjuic, Mariano Fortuny y Madrazo sees a grand theater raised in the sky. A theater of sky.

The girl steps into 509 Madison Avenue and asks for a Mariano Fortuny Delphos gown: a gown of white pleated silk to attire a deceased girl. The living girl emerges from 509 Madison Avenue and walks off resolutely. There is a European backdrop of ash-covered cities, fumid with Hitlerian soot. The living girl, the girl who walks with the package containing the Fortuny gown through the vicinity of Madison Avenue, had descended the staircase of the transatlantic liner one morning in April, in a dark violet dress and sheer silk leggings and a green blouse with flounces, her hair brushed into a bun and her baggage full of shawls and wool coats and gloves wrapped in white silk paper. With a revolver, the baroness was watching the movements of the body of the lover on the transatlantic liner. The living girl, Sapphic, dresses the dead girl, a suicide, who had watched her descend the staircase of the vessel in the April light, wrapping her in the Fortuny gown of white and pleated silk that clings to the whiteness of the sacrificed body. Mary McCarthy sees the suicide plunging through the raw white air while an airplane hums past overhead. In the garden of the Palazzo Vernier dei Leoni, Peggy Guggenheim, in a rippling Fortuny gown, walks with Mary McCarthy through the transparent oddments of the ruins of Marchesa Casati's extinguished forest. In the palace's picture gallery, the sky of liquid desires, painted by Dalí, is of a clear, washed-out blue, with a deeper blue in the heights. Beneath the arch of the long outspread arm in the blue cavalry jacket with golden epaulettes, brandishing a glimmering saber, the battle of Tétouan, painted by Mariano Fortuny y Marsal, is an apparition of mingled djellabas in white, blue, and yellow, and jet-black muskets on the canvas, again, painted by Dalí. The liquid desires, beneath the broad blue sky, are born in yellow viscera with blue hollows of caverns in a prairie of even green. Tétouan gleams on the horizon of a sacred blue sky.

Toward June of 1919, on the Boulevard Hausmann, close to the Opéra, there is a jab of gardened green. Clouds in the air: pollen from the chestnut blossoms. The porters come and go from number 98; choking on pollen, Marcel Proust leaves the room. He takes two steps, three; on the corner, in the shop window of Liberty's, he sees a Fortuny caftan of patterned velvet and a Fortuny burnoose of black silk stamped in gold, with a Tiepolo pink lining and pomegranate motifs. In the glass, the reflection of Marcel Proust forms a single color with the clouds of pollen and the white and blue and gilt of the Paris sky.

Incursions

The inhabitants of Mars arrive, in the whirlwind of autumn, in the outskirts of New Jersey. The inhabitants of Mars have descended from the black sky on a glimmering meteorite. With deadly ray guns, the inhabitants of Mars lay siege to a New York night the color of the velvet lining of a glove. From New York to Philadelphia, the interstates are choked with insectivore cars like metallic shooting stars. In New Jersey, the people flee through the streets to escape the suffocating gasses, covering their faces with damp rags. The murderous green Martians descend on Fifth Avenue; in a fluvial apocalyptic light, on a submarine night of smoking tar, men and women from New York tumble into the East River, oily and argentine. In the radio studios at CBS, in front of a black and white microphone, Orson Welles, in shirtsleeves, has his collar unbuttoned, with a loose, twisted tie bearing a pattern of asteroid-like dots. The entire floor is covered in empty paper cups for the drinking of sweet syrups and subdued, steaming coffees that come from a machine that makes an automated whirr. In one swig, Orson Welles empties a bottle of pineapple juice, then adjusts his headphones and orders the studio's orchestra to tear into the silk of Tchaikovsky's piano concerto. Shooting stars across a steel-blue night sky, shooting stars on the streets with their electrical clarity. Orson Welles's voice burns the microphone on the Martian night.

Orson Welles's voice, beneath the wood beams of the Palazzo Orfei, asks for sixteenth-century attire for the tragedy of Othello, the Moor of Venice. The winter is frosted silver in the house's amber windows. In gelid January, in February, piercing, purple, and impetuous, there is nothing inside to hinder the smothering of the tapestries. The face of Mariano Fortuny y Madrazo, under a blanket of white hair, is furrowed and scorched and tilled with hoes and plowshares. Mariano Fortuny y Madrazo rises, fatigued, and disappears into an unknown room. His arms full of gowns, Mariano Fortuny y Madrazo offers Orson Welles a doublet of green-grey brocade, lined with grey fur with spots of white. Orson Welles rises, opening and closing the doublet, sees, in the depths of the mirror, the soft reverberation of its lining, the color of pearl and quicklime. It is the fur of Australian moles, carnivores; the fur of moles with gnashing teeth that devour one another in the febrile Australian night. The evening has gone dark; Mariano Fortuny and Orson Welles no longer see each other's faces in the cottony shadows of velvet fabric in the Palazzo Orfei.

The Tragedy

In the courtyard of the ducal palace in 1938, the tragedy of
Othello, with Fortuny costumes, comes alive in sheets of
light that slice the shadow of the whitish stone. A djellaba
from the Orient, a green and coffee-colored Venetian gown,
a red dress with red leggings and no belt, a white and grey
tunic that shimmers with tremors of the lyre beneath the
marble of the giants' staircase. Othello and Desdemona,
at the height of 1949, take shelter beside a column of red
granite. Orson Welles looks into the sky; Desdemona, the
blonde, looks at the ground. At an angle, the campanile of
San Marco navigates the sea of transparent lamps, beaten by
the wings of a large flock of doves lost amid the glimmering
piazza's windblown pallor. Othello is a silk velvet doublet cre-
ated by Mariano Fortuny: over the very smooth white of the
backdrop, there are patterns of flowers, very pale green, and
motifs of a soft pumpkin red, and Turkish patterns from the
nineteenth century, pomegranate purple and very vivid for
the black-and-white camera of Orson Welles (the wheezing
reel in the projection room hurling a smoky halo of scattered
light toward the screen). Othello is a silk velvet doublet cre-
ated by Mariano Fortuny, with long, ample sleeves, decorated
with fur lining on the collar and cuffs, all dyed with carmine,
stamped with gold and pomegranate motifs in the style of

the year 1400 (Iago glides over a wind-swept trail at the feet of a tower where a large, empty cage is suspended). Othello is a silk velvet doublet created by Mariano Fortuny, stamped with gold and silver, with cotton pleats, with a white neck, white borders, white elbows and designs of copper, fleeting pink, and the darkest of greens. Orson Welles, bearded, in a cuirass, stands in profile before a round mirror. Orson Welles takes the camera in both hands. Othello takes the camera to film the tragedy of Othello. Othello is draped in a long white cape, knotted at the neck, open at the breast, in the room lined with columns. Desdemona lies in the shelter of the damasks, in the whiteness of her canopied death bed. In the sceno-graphic night of Venice, the sky of the Piazza San Marco is a storm of cinnamon, garnet, and pink, of carmine flashes in a glow of mauve clouds. Othello and Desdemona, beneath the gothic arches, are two lone figures against the undulating sky of cottony clouds at sea. Desdemona, in her marriage bed, is waiting for Othello. Her face is white, against the absolute black of the room. Othello is nothing but the horror in the depths of the eye of Orson Welles in the dark.

The Second of May

In Madrid, in November of 1867, Federico de Madrazo and
Mariano Fortuny y Marsal are looking at two large canvasses.
The air in the Paseo del Prado is a lingering majesty of faded
gold. The wind from the mountains splits apart against the
edges of the houses, blowing down the Carrera de San Jerón-
imo. On May 2, 1808, the air is sundrenched, with a shading
of broom; in the Carrera de San Jerónimo, the Mamelukes
on horseback in the portal of the Duke of Híjar's palace shoot
their harquebuses at the white-haired gatekeeper, stained with
blood, on the threshold. The volumes, the massed riders, twist
like helices. The Mamelukes wear white turbans, or turbans
with a band of white and a band of red, and breeches of bright
red or a muddy, earthen color that gives off a reddish gleam,
and smocks of deep blue or darkened green or a pink that
cedes to white. The Mamelukes ride white coursers. They
brandish daggers and scimitars, the hooves of their horses
tread the bloodied bodies before the grey-pink, bloodless
façades of the buildings beneath a sky without clarity, with
the matte reflectiveness of zinc.

The night is penitential: in a blue steeped in blackness,
against the background of a bell tower's conic steel peak, the
ruin is gilded and green. Standing before Goya's masterpiece,
they step back a few feet, Federico de Madrazo and Mariano

Fortuny y Marsal, in the museum's palatial, funereal light. The harquebusiers are a bundle of bayonets above the outraged gold of the soil with its underbrush of blood. The man about to be shot by the riflemen is wearing yellow breeches and a white, unbuttoned smock, his raised arms are outspread, his curled hair is the color of soot. The man about to be shot by the riflemen has an earthen face and coal in his eyes. On May 2, 1949, the Venetian back alley, clasped between shards of Byzantine sun, lights up the stained glass with a glow like an ambered bottle's. The sky is orange. Mariano Fortuny y Madrazo opens his eyes wide to stare at death.

The Bell

We hear the bell, but we do not see it. In the foreground, the white mitre of the presbyter in profile. The bell inhabits and uninhabits the Venetian streets. The pealing of the bell captivates the pavers that throb with mossy green beneath the tide; the sky is bleached with light, with a white or leaden swatch, a snatch of Washi paper clouds. The members of Desdemona's funeral train, stepping in a slow diagonal over sloping stones, brush past the mitre's white splendor, in cowls and gowns and long black capes like the wings of vultures. A chiaroscuro sheet hangs down from the litter bearing the deceased. They come there, the bell of San Marco, the bell of San Moisè, in the exequial morning of Mariano Fortuny y Madrazo, from the grand piazza, leaden with cupolas, from the secret piazza in the refuge of the canal, their echo pounding over the reflections of walls, of the visions of façades submerged in the trembling waters. In the mute rooms of the Palazzo Orfei, the machine for demonstrating Fortuny's system of indirect lighting shows a small-scale model of mountainous terrain: a craggy Valhalla, and now, in the background, above the escarpments the dark color of copper, an effervescence of white clouds invades a sky of lilac smoke, then bathes the boulders and the firmament in ocherous splendor with its rays of diffuse, inflamed white.

On Thursday, February 25, 1982, Orson Welles has arrived
in Paris. His hair, his beard, and his moustache waver between
silver and black. He is wearing a scarf with a pattern of white
dots, knotted loosely around his neck, and he walks, dressed
all in black, the Havana cigar between his lips smoking vig-
orously like the stack of a locomotive, resting the weight of
his body on a cane with an engraved handle. They follow
him to a large British car with French plates, parked, with the
door on the left-hand side open: a Bentley from the thirties,
manufactured by Rolls Royce, solemnly dark and reflective:
gleaming and black, with the steering wheel on the left, and
a high roof, so you may drive to the Ascot racecourse wear-
ing your top hat. On the car's metal and glistening leather
roof, the light of the Paris sky is reflected: inverted, aquatic,
a turbulent vanishment of trunks and branches of chestnuts.

The Japanese Salon

Henriette Fortuny's hair is white. It curls, corkscrews, effervesces like bells; her hair is a champagne crest like the maritime manes of the flower maidens. In the eyes of the young Mariano Fortuny y Madrazo, every woman was a crest of tousled hair. Henriette Fortuny is seated on a sofa with silk velvet cushions, beside a pedestal with a wooden base, supporting the white paper shade of a lit lamp. Behind the white helmet of Henriette Fortuny's hair breathes a painting in oil: the hand of a woman in a silk and satin skirt, in a frame with gilded moldings. On Henriette Fortuny's face, as she reads a book with ancient pages in the soft, collapsing remnants of the room, the passage of time has been a brief brushstroke: beneath her eyes, on her cheeks, on the curved creases in the flesh above her lips. In the ample chambers of the Palazzo Orfei, peopled with sylvan damasks, the piqué clarity of the azure spring of 1960 finds Henriette alone, leafing through an open album, with the mahogany perfume of prints against a backdrop of Ottoman cushions.

The wall of the Japanese salon is pale blue and dwindling green. In Rome, in 1874, in the Japanese salon of the residence of Mariano Fortuny y Marsal, the vegetation is an effulgence of tropical green vines, feverish with malaria, and white flowers that burst open like ears of grain and incubate a sanguine spark of red carnations. The sofa unfurls a vinous extravagance, dotted with black and vermillion. Near the girl's head, which rests on a blood-red cushion, is a tree in Chinese ink with two butterflies in ashen gold. The girl plays with a fan, white, pink, and ashen; she wears a white dress with a pink band around the waist, and white shoes. Reconquest of light in the Japanese salon. The boy – Mariano Fortuny y Madrazo – is an ivory nude with blond hair against the faded, dying blue of the wall. He is wrapped, from the waist down, in a sheet of deep blue festooned with red. The spectator's eye strays into the blue of the depths, so tenuous it dies into subtler green, and into the dissolution of all color.

Venice – Paris – Barcelona,
August 28 – December 7, 1982.

TO THE HAPPY FEW

Dramatis Personae

MARIANO FORTUNY, sculptor and exhibitor of wax figures.

MARIANO FORTUNY Y MARSAL, painter, grandson of the above.

CECILIA DE MADRAZO, wife of the above.

MARIANO FORTUNY Y MADRAZO, their son. Painter, photographer, scenographer, lighting technician, inventor, printmaker, entrepreneur, clothing designer.

HENRIETTE DE FORTUNY, née Henriette Negrin. Wife of Mariano Fortuny y Madrazo.

FEDERICO DE MADRAZO, painter. Father of Cecilia de Madrazo.

RAIMUNDO DE MADRAZO, painter. Son of the above.

COCO (FEDERICO) DE MADRAZO, painter. Son of Raimundo.

HENRY JAMES, novelist.

JOHN SINGER SARGENT, painter.

THE CURTIS FAMILY, distant relatives of the above and owners of the Palazzo Barbaro, where Sargent and James reside in Venice.

JEFFREY ASPERN, A YOUNG WOMAN, AN OLD LADY, AND A COLLECTOR OF RARE AUTOGRAPHS: characters in a novel by Henry James.

ROBERT BROWNING, poet.

RICHARD WAGNER, composer and poet.

PARSIFAL THE KNIGHT, THE FLOWER MAIDENS, TRISTAN AND ISOLDE, THE WARRIOR, AND THE VALKYRIE: Wagnerian beings.

FRANZ LISZT, composer, pianist, and ecclesiastic.

COSIMA WAGNER, née Cosima von Bülow, wife of Richard Wagner, daughter of Franz Liszt.

GABRIELE D'ANNUNZIO, writer of poetry and prose.

ELEONORA DUSE, tragedienne.

DRAMATIS PERSONAE

PRINCESS OF HOHENLOHE, owner of the Casetta Rossa, former sculpting studio of Canova.

REYNALDO HAHN, composer.

FRANCESCA DA RIMINI, historical tragic heroine and later character in Dante and D'Annunzio.

ÉMILIENNE D'ALENÇON, actress and courtesan.

THE YOUNG DUKE OF UZÈS, her deceased lover.

MARCEL PROUST, man of the world and, later, writer.

MIMY FRANCHETTI, Venetian aristocrat.

LIANE DE POUGY, actress, courtesan, and later wife of the Romanian prince Georges Ghika.

LIANE DE RECK, *nom-de-guerre* of a novice courtesan.

HENNESSY, sensual and senile aristocrat.

WOMEN FROM A BORDELLO, and a PORTER, actors in a clandestine film recorded by D'Annunzio.

MODELS FOR PHOTOGRAPHS AND PAINTINGS BY MARIANO FORTUNY Y MADRAZO, UNNAMED.

AN EGYPTIAN GIRL, model for John Singer Sargent.

A YOUNG LADY FROM NEW YORK WEARING A FORTUNY DRESS.

HUGO VON HOFMANNSTHAL, writer of poetry and prose.

HERR VON N., character in a novel by Hofmannsthal.

A PAINTER DISGUISED IN THE GOWN OF PETER PAUL RUBENS, not named in the text: Hans Makart, who strolled through Vienna in this manner in the year 1873.

GIACOMO CASANOVA, later known as Seingalt, Venetian adventurer.

HENRIETTE, one of his lovers.

MAX REINHARDT, theater director.

ALBERTINE, character in a novel by Marcel Proust, in reality his chauffeur Agostinelli.

ISABELLA, character in D'Annunzio, in reality the Marchesa Casati.

MARCHESA CASATI, extravagant aristocrat, owner of the Palazzo Vernier dei Leoni.

A MODEL FOR A PHOTOGRAPH IN A FORTUNY GOWN IN THE PALAZZO BARBARO.

ANTOINE, uranist hairdresser, AND HIS BELOVED.

BENITO MUSSOLINI, Duce.

ADOLF HITLER, Führer.

DRAMATIS PERSONAE

THE COUNTESS OF BÉARN, patroness.

FRANÇOISE, character in a novel by Proust.

ENRICO CARUSO, opera singer.

CHARLES SPENCER CHAPLIN, actor and film director.

MARC, son of Liane de Pougy, aviator, killed during the First World War.

MADAME DU BARRY, aristocrat and later film character portrayed by
Dolores del Río.

DOLORES DEL RÍO, Mexican aristocrat and later Hollywood actress.

ORSON WELLES, actor and director for stage, radio, and film.

AN UNNAMED STUDIO PHOTOGRAPHER: GEORGES HURRELL, who
began as a painter on the beaches of Malibu.

GEORGES SIMENON, novelist.

HENRY MILLER, writer.

OONA CHAPLIN, née O' Neill, last wife of Charles Spencer Chaplin.

GERALDINE CHAPLIN, actress, daughter of Charles Spencer Chaplin
and Oona O' Neill.

RUDOLPH VALENTINO, Italian actor in Hollywood.

NATACHA RAMBOVA, actually Winifred Hudnut, born in Salt Lake
City, actress, ballerina, and fashion designer, married for a time to
Rudolph Valentino.

ALLA NAZIMOVA, Russian actress and scriptwriter in Hollywood.

LILLIAN AND DOROTHY GISH, sisters, actresses in Hollywood.

DAVID WARK GRIFFITH, film director.

A LADY SEATED ON A STONE BENCH AT THE ALHAMBRA: wife of the
painter Joaquim Agrassot.

A PERSON IN A SOFT FELT HAT WATCHING A CARD GAME: the painter
Joaquim Agrassot, friend of Mariano Fortuny y Marsal.

ACTORS IN THE COURTYARD OF THE CASTELLO SFORZESCO:
Milanese aristocrats.

JULIE CHRISTIE, film actress.

AN UNNAMED GIRL, LESBIAN; HER LOVER, A BARONESS; AND A
SUICIDE LYING IN REPOSE: characters from a novel by Mary McCarthy.

MARY MCCARTHY, novelist.

PEGGY GUGGENHEIM, art collector, later owner, after the Marchesa
Casati, of the Palazzo Vernier dei Leoni.

INHABITANTS OF MARS AND AMERICAN CITIZENS IN PANIC: fictitious
and real characters brought into being by the radio adaptation,

directed and voiced by Orson Welles, of the H.G. Wells novel *War of the Worlds* in 1938.

OTHELLO, IAGO, DESDEMONA: characters in Shakespeare and Orson Welles. Othello is Welles himself.

THE MAMELUKES, THE DEAD BY FIRING SQUAD: figures from history and later in Goya.

THE PORTER OF THE DUKE OF HÍJAR, historical figure.

A GIRL BY THE WALL IN GRANADA AND IN THE JAPANESE SALON, UNNAMED: the sister of Mariano Fortuny y Madrazo.